Is Their Friendship Over?

"Why did you put this poor snake in my hiking boot?"
he asked.

"I didn't. I m-mean—" she stammered, not wanting
to tell him that Terri had been the one to put the snake
in there.

"You put a book on top of it, and he could've suffocated," Howard said accusingly.

"I would think he'd die from the smell first," she
said, wanting to laugh.

"That's not funny," said Howard. "Sometimes
you're the stupidest person I know, Sonya. You don't
care about anything that's worth caring about."

Sonya's eyes widened in horror. *"Me?* What about
you? What about the way you've been acting toward
me? You don't care about anything at all! You got your
wish. We aren't friends anymore!"

Books by Susan Smith

Samantha Slade: Samantha Slade: Monster Sitter
Samantha Slade: Confessions of a Teen-age Frog
Samantha Slade: Our Friend: Public Nuisance #1
Samantha Slade: The Terrors of Rock and Roll

Available from ARCHWAY Paperbacks

Best Friends #1: Sonya Begonia and the Eleventh Birthday Blues
Best Friends #2: Angela and the King-Size Crusade
Best Friends #3: Dawn Selby, Super Sleuth
Best Friends #4: Terri the Great
Best Friends #5: Sonya and the Chain Letter Gang
Best Friends #6: Angela and the Greatest Guy in the World
Best Friends #7: One Hundred Thousand Dollar Dawn
Best Friends #8: The Terrible Terri Rumors
Best Friends #9: Linda and the Little White Lies
Best Friends #10: Sonya and the Haunting of Room 16A
Best Friends #11: Angela and the Great Book Battle
Best Friends #12: Dynamite Dawn *vs*. Terrific Terri
Best Friends #13: Who's Out to Get Linda?
Best Friends #14: Terri and the Shopping Mall Disaster
Best Friends #15: The Sonya and Howard Wars

Available from MINSTREL Books

Best Friends™

#15 The Sonya and Howard Wars

by
Susan Smith

A MINSTREL® BOOK

PUBLISHED BY POCKET BOOKS

New York   London   Toronto   Sydney   Tokyo   Singapore

A MINSTREL PAPERBACK *ORIGINAL*

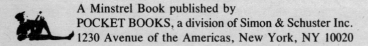

A Minstrel Book published by
POCKET BOOKS, a division of Simon & Schuster Inc.
1230 Avenue of the Americas, New York, NY 10020

Copyright © 1991 by Susan Smith

ISBN: 0-671-72490-8

First Minstrel Books printing August 1991

10 9 8 7 6 5 4 3 2 1

A MINSTREL BOOK and colophon are registered trademarks of Simon & Schuster Inc.

Cover art by Bill Donahey

Printed in the U.S.A.

*For Pamela Romero
and Cory Mendonca*

Chapter One

"Oh, John, I love you."

"I love you, too, Rose."

The hero and heroine moved closer together. Sonya Plummer leaned forward in her seat, her eyes glued to the movie screen. Suddenly Howard Tarter, the boy she was with, slid a skinny arm across the back of her chair. Then his hand dropped onto her shoulder.

Sonya was happily surprised. She turned to look at Howard, but he was staring straight ahead as though nothing had happened. Sonya reached up and touched his hand on her shoulder.

"Sonya, stop tickling me," Howard whispered. He slid his arm away and grabbed her hand.

The warmth of his smooth hand in hers made it hard for Sonya to concentrate on the movie. She did get involved again when the couple on the screen started kissing. She wished she and Howard were kissing, too. He smelled so good close to her like

1

that, like the super delicious chocolate double fudge cake that they'd eaten at her house before they went to the movies. She smiled, remembering that he'd asked her for the recipe.

When the credits started rolling, Howard leaned even closer to her. Sonya moved her head slightly so that she bumped Howard's glasses, and the kiss Howard started to give her landed on the side of her nose.

But it was a *kiss!* Not exactly a movie kiss, but who cared? Sonya couldn't believe it!

"Finally!"

"I thought we were going to camp right here!" exclaimed Terri Rivera, hoisting her bright orange backpack onto her shoulder after kissing her mom and dad and sister, Lia.

"I'm already pooped, and we haven't hiked an inch yet," said Angela King, pushing a lock of curly brown hair behind a rolled red bandanna. Her mom had had to leave, so Mrs. Rivera gave her a hug and kiss, too.

All around them girls rose from a jumble of bedrolls and suitcases. A big beat-up bus with "Camp Long River" painted on the side turned into Banner Junior High School's parking lot, where parents and campers had been waiting for more than an hour.

A large woman wearing baggy blue jeans, a Camp Long River sweatshirt, and a whistle on a lanyard around her neck got off the bus. She signaled to the girls, blew her whistle, and shouted, "*All aboard for*

Camp Long River! Please have your permission slips in hand!"

"Come on," said Sonya after a quick hug for her mom. She was the first to have her stuff ready to board the bus. Her bedroll was bonking her in the head, her backpack straps were too tight and pulling at her light brown hair, and her suitcase was knocking against her knees as she started for the bus.

Her best friends, Terri Rivera, Angela King, Dawn Selby, and Monique Whitney, followed close behind her.

"Hi, I'm Nadia," said the woman, smiling at the girls as they handed her their permission slips.

"Hi," the girls chorused.

"Leave your packs and suitcases over there. They'll go in the baggage compartment under the bus," Nadia instructed.

"What a relief!" groaned Dawn, who was the second smallest of the group. Her suitcase was almost as big as she was.

Monique, a tiny black girl, looked like a skinny little weight lifter as she hefted her huge suitcase. She wouldn't let her father help her at all.

The five friends squashed their packs together on the asphalt and hopped on the bus to take seats together at the back.

"Someone told me the food at camp is gross," said Angela, wrinkling her nose. Angela loved food but was always dieting. Her mom was a critic for a food magazine.

"It's not that bad," said Sonya. "Anyway, camp has other advantages."

"Like seeing Howard, for instance?" asked Angela.

"You only wanted to come this year because of Howard," said Terri, pushing a hand through her spiky, short dark hair.

"I did not. I went to camp before," insisted Sonya.

"Yeah, when you were eight years old," Terri said. "You were barely toilet-trained."

Sonya stared down at her faded and tight Camp Long River T-shirt and felt foolish that she'd worn it. "I'm sure it'll be fun, with or without Howard," she said, her face warm.

"It won't be the same as when you were little," Terri said, staring at the T-shirt logo stretched tight across Sonya's expanded chest.

Sonya did have to admit it was true that she had wanted to go because Howard was going to Camp Honeywell. The boys' camp was just a short distance down the river from Camp Long River.

"I'm sure camp's going to be really romantic this time—with Howard nearby," said Angela, winking.

Sonya knew she had been thinking of nothing but romance since she decided to go to camp. She dreamed of sitting beside Lake Pinecrest with Howard, singing songs and looking at the stars. Especially after they had had that great movie date before camp.

The bus to Camp Long River zoomed along the freeway, filled with shouting, singing girls. The open windows let in the fresh, pine-scented air. Sonya turned and noticed that Dawn was quiet and probably homesick. She knew her friend would love camp eventually, but it would take her a little longer to adjust.

Someone started singing "Ten Green Bottles Hanging on the Wall," and everyone joined in.

"I wish Linda and Jennifer could've come," said Sonya. Two more of the best friends, Linda Carmichael and Jennifer Soo, had had to stay home.

"Yeah, me, too," said Terri. "But Linda wanted to make some money this summer."

"And Jennifer was looking forward to spending the summer with her dad," added Angela.

Finally the bus pulled off onto a dirt road. The girls were bounced around so much that they had to stop singing.

As they drew closer to camp, Sonya's excitement grew. A sharp drop on one side of the road took her breath away, just as it had the first time she came to camp. A doe bounded through the woods and disappeared as quickly as she had appeared.

Suddenly, through the pines, Sonya glimpsed a shimmering blue sliver of lake between the straight tree trunks. A big, carved redwood sign over a gravel drive said: "Camp Long River." A homemade banner fluttered down from the sign and said, "Welcome to Camp Long River!"

"We're here!" cried Sonya, pressing her nose against the glass.

"No, I thought we were at Disneyland," Terri said sarcastically.

"It almost looks like it could be one of the exhibits at Disneyland," said Dawn, staring at the group of girls lined up beside the road who waved as the bus rumbled by.

When the bus stopped, everyone scrambled to get out before anyone else.

Terri was so impatient, she was ready to mow down anyone ahead of her.

"Hey, let's just wait until everyone gets off," said Dawn. "What's the big rush?"

"Yeah," said Monique, slipping back into her seat to wait.

Finally they got off the bus. Sonya and her friends retrieved their stuff and joined the large group of girls headed for the dining room.

Sonya pointed out the sights. "The camp is located right where Lake Pinecrest and Long River come together. Oh, and there's a tiny little island in the middle of Long River."

"Where's the boys' camp, Sonya?" asked Angela.

"Just a short boat trip downriver thataway," said Sonya, pointing.

"Is that all you guys think about?" asked Dawn.

All the buildings were built of logs, just as Sonya had remembered, but they looked so much smaller! They took one of the many dirt trails to the dining room, which was just a large log cabin with rows of trestle tables.

Once everyone was seated the camp director, Mr. Thompson, had name tags handed out to everyone. He welcomed the girls, went over the rules of the camp, and introduced the staff. Finally he turned the meeting over to one of the counselors.

"Hi, I'm one of the counselors, Merrie Jackson." She smiled prettily. She had a Southern accent and long blond hair that fell over her shoulders like spun gold and showed off her tan. Sonya thought she was beautiful.

"How many of you have been to Camp Long River before?" asked Merrie, tugging at the hem of her cute purple shorts suit.

Sonya really liked nice clothes and suddenly wished she wasn't wearing her dumb little, too-tight T-shirt. She raised her hand in response to Merrie's question, along with about thirty other kids.

"Maybe when you have time you old-timers can show the others around and answer any of their questions," suggested Merrie. "Now, next on the agenda is to find out which cabin you'll be in. We've divided you up into groups of four girls to a cabin."

"Four!" cried Monique.

"That's right," drawled Merrie, smiling at Monique. She started reading off groups of four and assigning them cabins. Merrie read off Sonya's, Terri's, Angela's, and Monique's names and said that they'd be together and she'd be their counselor. One counselor was assigned to eight girls. Merrie would be sleeping in the other cabin because those girls were younger.

"But what about me?" cried Dawn, tears springing into her big blue eyes. Her name tag was on upside down.

"You'll be with another group," said Merrie, introducing her to three tall girls. One of the girls, with short red hair and green, catlike eyes, stared at Dawn.

"I'm Lauren Tompkins," she said to Dawn. Dawn cringed.

"This is the worst," whispered Sonya.

"Of all people to get separated from us," groaned Angela.

"She'll cry a river," said Terri.

"Can't we work it out so Dawn can be with us?" Sonya asked Mr. Thompson.

"Let's try it this way for now," he said gently but firmly. "You'll all have some free time after you get settled in. Please wander around and get your bearings."

Sonya felt sick. She was sure Dawn, who got very homesick, was going to have trouble with this arrangement, but there was nothing they could do about it yet.

When the meeting was over, the girls, minus Dawn, trudged over to their cabin, Cabin 4. There were four bunks and four bureaus in the room and a small closet. There was also one tiny bathroom with only a sink and a toilet for all four girls.

"I sure hope we don't all have to go to the bathroom at the same time," said Angela after they were all unpacked.

"Come on. Let's go get Dawn and look at the lake," said Terri, who ran outside before anyone could disagree.

Sonya and the others followed and met Dawn almost instantly running toward them, crying.

"Is it that bad?" asked Sonya.

"It's worse," sniffled Dawn, wiping her nose with her sleeve. "There's one awful girl named Lauren, a redhead. She bosses me around and makes fun of me. I swear, I won't be able to sleep with her in the same room."

"Maybe we can work something out," said Sonya. But she didn't know what.

"How? There are only four bunks in each cabin," said Monique.

They were now at the water's edge, and small sailboats zipped across the calm blue lake. There were a lot more people than Sonya remembered from her first camp stay.

All at once Dawn bent over at the waist and threw up.

"Oh, no, are you okay?" asked Sonya, rubbing her friend's back.

Dawn couldn't reply for a while. Finally she said, "That Lauren makes me totally sick."

"Maybe you have a virus," suggested Monique, who knew a lot about health problems. She offered Dawn a tissue and suggested she get a drink of water.

"This Lauren sounds like a disease, if you ask me," said Terri as the girls made their way back from the lake. She stomped on up to the cabins.

"Hey, where are you going?" asked Sonya.

"I'm going to find someone to yell at and tell them

to move Dawn into our cabin!" Terri shouted over her shoulder.

Sonya, Monique, Angela, and Dawn followed. They searched all over and finally found Merrie in the kitchen. Dawn stood just outside the screen door because she thought she'd infect the food. The kitchen, with its big stainless steel appliances, reminded Sonya of Dawn's family bakery back home.

"I think she should stay with us. She can share my bed," Terri was saying. "She's sick and she'll feel better with us."

They all trooped outside, where Merrie studied Dawn's pale face. "Okay, she can stay with you but just for tonight. She'll probably be feeling better tomorrow, right, Dawn? Probably just all the excitement."

"Yeah, probably," said Dawn, trying to smile.

That night at dinner Dawn couldn't eat but didn't want to stay in the cabin alone. She listlessly pushed her food around on her plate.

"I can't eat, either, and I'm not even sick," said Angela. "The peas were cooked for at least ten years."

"And the meat is like mush," added Sonya.

"This isn't even a good time to be a vegetarian," said Terri, who was a vegetarian when she felt like being one.

"Try the salad," suggested Monique. "They can't mess that up very much."

They all stared at it and said all together, "Oh, yes, they can." The salad consisted of large lettuce leaves with a few tomato hunks thrown in, and the whole thing was drowning in a thick mayonnaise dressing.

"I think I'm going to barf again," moaned Dawn.

"Keep it up, and you'll get to stay in our cabin for the whole session," said Sonya eagerly.

Terri frowned. "I've never heard anyone get so excited about being sick before."

"Let's hurry and get out of here. Don't forget we have a campfire tonight," said Sonya. "With the boys from Camp Honeywell."

"Yuck," said Dawn. She still didn't like boys.

"Come on, Dawn. Maybe it'll take your mind off your stomach," said Angela.

They cleared off their plates and put them in a pile with all the other dirty dishes. Then the five girls trooped out to the campfire, picking up their ration of marshmallows, graham crackers, and chocolate bars that was to be their dessert that night.

"I haven't had S'mores since Brownie Scouts," said Dawn, plonking herself down on one of the large boulders that circled the fire.

"I hear they're the best thing for upset stomachs," said Angela and laughed.

Merrie was already there, giving a lesson to her other four charges on how to build a fire. Flames were already starting to flicker and dance in the cooler night air. The crackle of the fire was comforting to Sonya and the other girls.

Just when Sonya thought she couldn't wait another second, the boys from Camp Honeywell came hiking up the trail that circled the lake.

Sonya stood up to scan the group for Howard. Then she saw him, all skin and bones in long baggies and a polo shirt. With his small face hidden behind his thick-framed glasses, and his short hair sticking straight up, he looked like a little absentminded professor. And he was the smallest boy in the group!

"I don't know why, but Howard looks weird," said Sonya. All the other boys were big, athletic types, and they were wearing football jerseys and baseball caps.

"He looks like a fish out of water," said Angela.

"He definitely doesn't look happy," Dawn noted.

The girls sat on one side of the fire, while the boys sat directly across from them.

Sonya busied herself threading a marshmallow on a straightened wire coat hanger and hung it over the fire. Her friends did the same.

"Hey, don't we get any?" asked one of the biggest boys.

The counselors, who had been hopping to busily passing out some more makings to everyone, told the kid to cool it. They handed around more wire coat hangers and everyone began threading and roasting marshmallows. Everyone but Howard, who kept dropping his marshmallows into the fire.

Sonya finally got to her feet and crossed over to enemy territory to sit beside him. "Here, like this, Howard." She took a marshmallow and shoved it onto the hanger. "See? Make sure you stab the marshmallow right in the center. And just brown it, don't let it burn up or it just melts."

"Thanks, Sonya," said Howard. He was blushing, firelight reflected in his glasses.

The boys around him laughed and jabbed one another in the ribs.

"Hey, Howie, you need your girlfriend to help you do that?" one loud boy named Robbie shouted.

Robbie rolled in the dirt, clutching his stomach as he howled with laughter.

"Shut up!" cried Sonya, glaring at him.

Howard inched away from Sonya.

"Hey, Howie's got a girlfriend," chanted another boy, popping a perfectly browned marshmallow into his mouth.

"I hope you choke!" exclaimed Sonya.

Howard had moved over to stand in front of both boys, waving his marshmallow hanger in front of them. His face was beet red with anger. "Shut up! She's *not* my girlfriend!"

Sonya's mouth fell open. Her heart felt as if it had just dropped to her feet.

She stared at Howard in disbelief. Her eyes felt as if they could burn a hole through him. *"What?"*

Howard met her glance for a second, then shifted his gaze to the ground. All the boys began laughing at Sonya now.

Chapter Two

"Attention, campers!"

Sonya and her friends stopped talking to listen to Merrie's announcement. They were at the base of a trail, ready to go on a nature hike.

"We're going to identify wildflowers today. Right here beside my feet is the bighead clover," Merrie explained, pointing at a clump of pink flowers. "Now, if you're looking for a four-leaf clover, this is where you might find it. Some people cook and eat this clover."

Dawn and two other girls bent over to search for four-leaf clovers.

"Why do they call it bighead?" asked Dawn.

"Because it has a big flower head instead of the small one your lawn clover back home has," drawled Merrie. "Now, follow me. When you see something you recognize, I want y'all to shout out."

"I thought this was going to be a real hike, with bears and stuff," complained Terri.

"Maybe she's getting us ready for the hard stuff later," said Dawn, her eyes round with fear.

"I think I'd rather look at wildflowers," said Sonya.

"Yeah, me, too. I'm not ready to meet any bears," said Monique. "I wouldn't know what to say."

They trudged up the rocky path and stopped again so Merrie could point out the next plant.

"Oh, look! The boys!" exclaimed Angela.

Right ahead was a group from Camp Honeywell. Both boys' and girls' camps had been issued camp T-shirts, so they looked like teams. Sonya raised her eyes, not sure whether she wanted to see Howard after the night before.

"Hey, Jay! How y'all doin'?" Merrie called to the boys' counselor.

"Fine, Merrie. Howard here's teaching me a few things," Jay said, winking at her. He was tall and tanned with lots of curly dark hair pulled back in a ponytail.

"I think he likes her," Angela whispered in Sonya's ear.

"He'd be crazy not to," said Sonya. "Isn't she the most beautiful person you ever saw?"

"Yeah, and nice, too," replied Angela.

"He's cute, too," said Monique, squishing up close to the others.

Sonya noticed that all the girls were staring at Merrie and Jay as if they were major entertainment.

Then she noticed Howard, wearing a T-shirt that was at least three sizes too large for him. He was still talking to Jay even though Jay's attention was on Merrie.

"Well, lupines are part of the pea family," Howard was saying, craning his neck to stare into Jay's face.

"How about that?" Jay said, turning to include Howard.

"What a nerd," muttered Robbie, who was about five times Howard's size.

Another large boy pushed Robbie so he fell on top of the flowers Howard was describing.

"Stop that!" Howard exclaimed. "Do you know how long it takes for those plants to grow back after you trample them?"

"A thousand years?" asked Robbie, snickering.

"Just about," Howard said, suddenly furious. "These alpine plants are really fragile, and when they get damaged, it takes about ten years for them to grow back."

"Howard's right," Jay put in. "You guys stay on the trail, and stop horsing around." He moved on with Merrie.

"What are you? Some kind of save-the-plants guy or something?" taunted Robbie, giving Howard a shot with his elbow when Jay wasn't looking.

Howard seemed to be pretty miserable. Sonya stood within hearing distance and felt sorry for him.

"He doesn't have a single friend here," she said.

"Yeah, that's rough," said Terri.

"I can't stand it," said Sonya, breaking away from the group.

"Where are you going?" cried Dawn.

"Just watch!"

She stomped ahead, straight for the big guy, Robbie.

"You're one of those friends of trees, too, aren't you?" Robbie sneered, his face still pressed up close to Howard's, fogging his glasses.

Jay had moved farther up the trail still talking with Merrie and didn't see what was going on. Howard was trembling.

Sonya marched up to Robbie and yanked on his holey T-shirt. "You stop it!"

"What?" Robbie flicked her fingers off his shirt as if she were an annoying fly. "What's with you?"

She planted her hands on her hips. "Howard is the smartest person I know. You leave him alone. He's *not* a nerd."

All the boys doubled over with laughter, and Robbie just stood grinning down at her.

"Howie's girlfriend!" one of the boys chanted.

"Howie needs a *girl* to stick up for him!" cried Robbie.

"Dig this dumb girl!" somebody else hollered.

"Hey, Robbie, you wanna fight a girl?" another one said.

"Is she your girlfriend?" Robbie asked.

Howard was red all over. He shoved his hands deep in his pockets and brushed past Sonya, heading up the trail. "She's just a girl from my school back home," he said.

"What?" she screamed.

"Hey, what's going on down there?" cried Jay. "Come on, you guys, get on up here!"

"Sonya! Join us, please!" Merrie called out, waving her hands frantically.

Sonya couldn't believe it.

"I can't believe it," she whispered when she got back to her friends.

"What?"

"Didn't you hear?"

"No, what?" cried Dawn.

"He's acting like he hardly knows me, and we were supposed to be so close," said Sonya, fighting back tears.

"This was supposed to be a summer of romance for you," said Angela, lacing her arm through Sonya's.

"That stinks," said Terri, frowning. "You stuck up for him, Sonya, and that's how he treats you? Forget him!"

"Yeah, forget him!" cried Monique, who liked to copy Terri.

"I guess I'll have to," Sonya replied, but she felt awful. The day—and camp—was totally ruined for her now.

"Okay, I'm going to pair y'all off with a person you don't know so you can get to know new campers," said Merrie that afternoon.

Sonya and her friends had been sitting together by the lake after lunch. She studied the other girls, wondering who she'd get stuck with.

"Okay, Wanda and Sonya. Go over to the bulletin board and pick an activity," Merrie instructed.

Sonya stared up at a tall, stoop-shouldered girl with black, frizzy hair.

"I'm Wanda," she said uninterestedly.

"Hi, I'm Sonya," said Sonya, smiling up into Wanda's solemn face. "Let's go see what we can do."

"I hate it here, and I don't want to do anything," said Wanda, trudging along beside her.

"Come on. I'm sure there'll be something we both like," said Sonya. They stared at the big bulletin board on the outside of the dining hall.

There was horseback riding, swimming, basket weaving, sewing, lanyard making, tennis, croquet, Ping-Pong, hiking. . . .

"What're your favorites?" asked Sonya.

"I don't like anything," said Wanda. "Everything's boring."

Sonya sighed heavily. "Tell you what. I'm going to pick something with my eyes closed."

"Yeah?" Wanda said in the same bored tone of voice.

Sonya closed her eyes and pointed, hoping she'd get horseback riding. When she opened them, her finger was on basket weaving.

"Oh, great," said Wanda.

"I can pick again," said Sonya.

"Don't bother. Everything's awful anyway."

"At least we won't get dirty," said Sonya, leading the way to the arts and crafts cabin. After hiking she had changed into a pink and white T-shirt and white shorts.

When they walked in the door of the cabin, Sonya gasped.

She took in the scene: Plastic jars of paints lined the wooden shelves, on a table were clay sculptures drying, and off in a corner Howard was sitting at a table with a counselor. He was surrounded by grasses and reeds stuck in large pots of warm water.

"So this is the direction of your first weave—" said the instructor.

Howard saw Sonya and his mouth fell open. Looking embarrassed, his gaze dropped to the reeds he was beginning to work with. Sonya began sweating. He didn't even say hi when she and Wanda sat down across from him.

"Hi, girls. I'm DeeDee. Why don't you just listen and then I'll work with you on starting a project, okay?" said the counselor, whose bright orange hair made a halo around her tiny sunburned face.

Sonya searched the room for an escape. If only there were a hole in the floor she could drop through! But there she was—trapped between dull Wanda and horrible Howard for an entire hour of basket weaving!

Chapter Three

"I can't stand it!"

Dawn stood at the head of the breakfast table, her fine blond hair flat to her head, uncombed. There were dark circles under her eyes.

"What's wrong?" asked Sonya.

"Yeah, you look awful," said Monique.

Dawn slumped down at the table and stared at her bowl of cereal. The room was loud with the clatter of plates and silverware and the music of girls' voices.

"Lauren stole my night-light, and then they all sat around and told scary stories in the dark. I had nightmares, and they laughed at me because I was scared!"

"Oh, Dawn, that's awful!" cried Angela, wrapping an arm around her friend.

"What a creep that girl is!" exclaimed Terri, stabbing her grapefruit.

"Let's talk to Merrie—she's the nicest counselor—and let her know what's going on," said Sonya.

After breakfast the five girls marched over to the counselors' table and asked Merrie if they could speak to her.

"We have to tell you something," Sonya said when they had her alone.

"Will you just look at Dawn?" said Angela, pushing Dawn out in front of her.

Dawn made herself look as pathetic as possible.

"Have you ever seen anything like it?" asked Terri.

Merrie studied Dawn. "What's wrong, Dawn? Are you sick again?"

"I didn't sleep all night," she said mournfully. "The girls in Cabin Five are *awful!*"

"Dawn's afraid of the dark, and they took her night-light and told ghost stories to give her nightmares," explained Sonya. "So I was wondering if we could each take turns and stay in Five for a few days and then switch off. That way Dawn wouldn't have to stay there."

"What!" asked Terri.

"It's a good idea, Terri, so shut up," said Monique.

"But—"

Angela clamped a hand over Terri's mouth.

Merrie smiled at them. "I'll see what I can do. It might not be easy to get the camp director's permission. He likes to keep girls in the same cabins for the whole camp stay. That way we know where y'all are."

"Oh, please," said Sonya. Merrie quieted her by promising to do her best.

"Okay, campers!" the camp director shouted, clapping his hands and then resorting to his whistle. Girls clustered around. "Coming up today—in fact, in thirty minutes—we are going to begin our annual camp wars against the boys from Honeywell. Sign up for any contest you want to be a part of. But remember that the losers of any contest have to do the cleanup after that activity. So you don't want to lose!"

"Let's choose something we don't mind cleaning up after," suggested Angela.

"Or something we know we can win," said Terri.

"Something to do with horses," said Sonya.

"But that would mean mucking out stalls if we lost!" exclaimed Dawn.

"We definitely have to choose something we can win," said Terri.

"Yeah, what're we all good at?" asked Dawn.

"We all like horses and can ride," said Sonya. "Even Monique, now that she's taking that new allergy medicine, can ride." Sonya lived on a ranch and had horses of her own, and her friends often rode with her.

Everyone raced for the main bulletin board, where the contests were listed.

"Barrel races! Let's do that, Sonya!" yelled Monique.

Terri was the first to wriggle through the mob. She

wrote all five of their names down under Barrel Races.

"What's a barrel race?" asked Dawn as they walked away.

"It's a horseback race, where you ride around three barrels in a cloverleaf pattern, like this." Sonya hunkered down and lined up three stones in the dirt to represent barrels. Then she traced a twig around them. "See, you weave in and out of the barrels as fast as you can without knocking them over."

The girls ran to their cabins to change into jeans and then met outside to walk to the stables together.

"Oh, no! There's Howard," said Angela as they approached the stables.

"I wonder if we're going to be racing against his group?" asked Monique. Another team of girls from Camp Long River was already mounted.

"Looks like it," said Sonya. "There's one team of boys and girls already mounted. Hey, we'll take this easily if we're up against Howard."

The stables smelled of warm horse manure and sweet alfalfa hay. A couple of extra horses were tethered to a fence outside and whinnied a greeting when Sonya and her friends arrived. The girls patted them, and the horses nudged the girls with their velvety noses.

The first two teams rode out just then to the race area.

Robbie, who would be on the next team, saw Sonya and pointed her out to the other boys. "Hey, there's Howard's girlfriend!"

"Shut up, already!" cried Howard, scowling at Sonya.

Terri raised her fists to Robbie. "Ew, I'd like to punch your lights out."

Angela wrestled Terri's fists behind her back. "Cool it, Terri."

"How much you wanna bet we win?" Robbie asked Sonya. He was standing directly behind a horse that could kick at any moment.

Sonya reached over and tugged Robbie out of the way. "Watch out—you'll get kicked!" Seeing how ignorant he was about horses, she said, "I'm sure we'll win."

"Well, I'm an expert rider," said Robbie.

"Could've fooled me," noted Angela, hooting with laughter.

"And Howard's been on a horse a total of three times," added Sonya.

"How do you know that? I've ridden horses without you around, you know," Howard replied, his ears glowing red.

"Oh, yeah? Well, it never showed," said Sonya, glaring at him.

"I don't think I've ever hated boys this much in my entire life," said Angela.

"Yeah, I know what you mean," whispered Sonya. "Every time I see Howard now, I want to strangle him."

The first group of contestants had finished the race and cleared the ring. The boys had won.

Once Sonya's group was mounted on horseback,

Lonnie, the counselor in charge, gave them the instructions for the contest.

"Okay, each of you has to be ready to compete right after the girl or boy in front of you, like a relay. So you have to be ready to ride the minute your teammate charges through the gate. I'll clock your times. You'll ride as fast as you can in a cloverleaf pattern around the three barrels, up and back and out the gate. Times will be clocked from the moment you enter the paddock to the moment you leave it. If you knock over a barrel, five seconds will be added to your time. The girls will be first."

"I wish we had time to practice first," said Dawn.

"Don't worry. The guys won't be able to beat us, practice or no practice," said Sonya more confidently than she felt.

"Terri Rivera goes first."

Terri rode up to the open gate and hunched over her horse's neck. When the cap pistol sounded, she rode into the paddock, charging around the barrels at breakneck speed. At the last one, her horse kicked the barrel and knocked it over. But her time was so fast, it barely mattered, and everyone applauded wildly.

Dawn was next. She was a lightweight but rode fast and carefully, without knocking any barrels over. Next went Monique, who, because she hadn't been riding long, wasn't as good as the others, and her time was a couple of minutes slower. Angela went next. She rode well but knocked one barrel over.

Then it was Sonya's turn. She rode her horse hard

and fast, reining him in for the turns, just missing the barrels by a hair. Her time was the best for her team.

Robbie, the first boy up, urged his horse to go too fast. He knocked over two barrels. Three other boys, following his example, also didn't score well because they rode too fast. Howard's method was slow and steady, but still he couldn't control his horse.

In the middle of a turn Howard's horse reared, and he slid off and landed flat in the dust. Looking miserable, he dusted himself off and limped with his head bent as he led his horse back to the gate.

"Is he okay?" asked Sonya.

"Who cares?" said Terri. "He deserved to fall off."

"Okay. The obvious winner of that contest was Camp Long River!" announced Lonnie.

The girls whooped with joy.

"The losers get to muck out the stables!" cried Lonnie.

The boys stared at one another with identical, pained expressions. "Oh, no!"

"Hurray!" shouted the girls, locking their arms together for one giant hug.

Chapter Four

❀

Sonya covered her eyes.

"I can't watch."

"Wake me when it's over," said Angela.

"It's awful," said Monique.

"It's pathetic," said Terri.

"I hope he's not hurt," Dawn said worriedly.

They had been standing on the shore of Long River and just happened to see Howard fall headfirst out of his rowboat while trying to land a fish. His glasses flew off, of course, and he was now diving under water to search for them.

"He won't be able to find his glasses because he can't see without them," said Sonya and sighed.

The other boys had rowed their boats around Howard and were laughing at him.

"Hey, old Howie lost his glasses. What're you gonna do, Howie?" yelled Robbie.

"Somebody help me look for them, please!" Howard shouted, shivering as he clung to the side of his rowboat.

"I wish I could help," said Sonya. "But it would only make things worse."

"I'd like to drown that dumb Robbie," said Terri.

Reluctantly Sonya turned away from the scene and her friends followed her.

"Yesterday Howard came in last in the relay races, and he totally blew it in the baseball game, and now he's lost his glasses. Camp doesn't seem to be his thing."

"Face it, Sonya. Howard is not exactly a star athlete, and most camp stuff is athletic," Monique pointed out.

"He's got a lot of brains, though," said Sonya.

"Yeah, but the boys he's with don't have brains," said Angela.

"You can be athletic and smart at the same time," said Terri.

"Yeah, nobody ever said you had to be either one or the other," added Dawn.

They consulted the bulletin board outside the dining hall for their next activity, which would be against boys. They had a choice—tennis or archery.

"How about tennis?" asked Sonya. "Except I haven't played in a while."

"I'm terrible," said Dawn. "And I'm tired. Those dumb girls in my cabin kept me awake again last night." Unfortunately, the exchange idea hadn't been approved, so Dawn was still in Cabin 5.

"We're good enough even if you're tired," said Terri, playfully socking Monique on the arm.

"Ugh, I hate running after the balls," Angela said, groaning.

"Come on. If we get to play Howard, we'll win for sure," said Terri. She wrote their names down under Tennis.

After lunch Sonya and her friends met on the tennis courts. All except Terri and Monique, who had brought their own rackets, had to use unfamiliar ones, so they practiced hitting balls for a while before playing.

When the boys arrived, they slugged the balls across the net as though they were playing baseball. Howard hung back, looking miserable. But Sonya was happy to see he had his glasses back on his nose.

One part of Sonya was glad to see him so miserable, because he had made her so miserable. But another part felt sorry for him.

"Okay, we're ready!" yelled Robbie after two seconds of warm-ups.

Sonya exchanged glances with her friends. "Okay," she said nervously.

"Look, if we lose, it won't be bad," Dawn reasoned. "All we'll have to do is pick up balls."

"*And* clean the tennis room," added Angela.

Howard and a tall, thin boy named Maurice were Dawn and Sonya's opponents. They spun Sonya's racket to decide who would choose sides and first service. The boys called "rough" and won the spin.

Maurice served first. He had long, monkeylike arms, but his serve was weak, and he couldn't get the ball over the net. Throughout his whole serve no one got to swing at the ball once because it never went over.

"We won!" cried Sonya.

Next it was the girls turn to serve, and they had to change courts. Sonya was up first and got the ball over and in. Maurice, who returned, just plopped the ball back over the net.

Dawn returned it hard to the back court, and Howard fell over, landing on his hands and knees, trying to retrieve it.

"Our point!" crowed Sonya. She served again, and this time the boys couldn't even return it. She kept on serving, and the boys never returned another ball. The girls quickly won.

Next, Howard served. "The score is zero-two," he called. He threw the ball too high and then couldn't find it to hit it. Sonya began shouting instructions.

"Throw the ball a little in front of you and to the right. And keep your eye on it all the time you're serving."

Terri shook her head. "Don't help him."

Howard tried it, and his next serve sailed over the net and into the correct box. Sonya returned the ball hard and gained the point. Next time Howard did a little better. He served correctly and made a point.

"Uh-oh. They're waking up," said Dawn, crouching over her racket.

They ended that game with the boys getting one point. Dawn served next and won the game, game–15. That brought the score to 4–0, girls' favor. They won the next two games to put the set away.

When it was over, Sonya and Dawn walked up to the net and shook hands with Howard and Maurice.

"Nice game," said Sonya, grinning at Howard.

"Yeah, thanks," said Howard, but he wasn't grinning.

"You could use a couple of lessons, Howard," said Sonya, trying to be helpful.

"I know that." He sounded irritated.

"Aren't you going to congratulate us on our great game?" asked Dawn.

"Great game," said Maurice.

Howard glared at Sonya.

"Yeah. It's not every day I win a tennis game," said Sonya, bouncing a ball with her racket.

"Congratulations!" Howard yelled, then whirled around and stomped off the court.

Sonya watched him go, her spirits sinking.

"Boy, what a sore loser," said Dawn.

Terri, Angela, and Monique came over. They had won their doubles games, too.

"What did you ever see in him?" asked Angela.

"I can't remember," Sonya replied, not wanting to talk about it.

"He's definitely different than he is at home," said Terri. She twirled her racket up in the air.

"I could almost think he's a completely different person," said Monique. "Because that's how he's acting."

"Yeah. Except for the face and body, I'd say that's not Howard Tarter," said Dawn.

"How about this—some alien beings have taken over Howard's body and mind, so it's really them we're seeing and not Howard," suggested Angela.

"And the real Howard is in space somewhere, trapped in some alien body!" cried Dawn excitedly.

Terri shook her head. "You guys are losing it."

Thump! Thump! Thump!

Sonya awoke suddenly in the top bunk, bonking her head on the ceiling. What was that awful noise?

"Let me in!" cried a small voice.

Terri was awake and sitting bolt upright.

"It's Dawn!"

"Let her in!"

"It's two in the morning!"

By that time all four girls were wide-awake and scrambling out of their bunks. They crowded around the door and fumbled with the latch.

"The door was stuck," said Terri, opening the door wide.

"What's wrong?" asked Sonya, taking a trembling Dawn into her arms.

Dawn broke away and started scratching herself all over frantically.

"What happened?" cried Monique sleepily.

"Those girls," Dawn spluttered, then burst into

fresh tears. "It was Lauren's idea. They put spiders in my bed! They must have spent all day collecting them, and then after I was asleep, they dropped them in and I woke up with spiders crawling all over me. When I started screaming, they just laughed at me!"

She started sobbing all over again.

"Dawn, it's okay now," soothed Sonya. She handed her a tissue, and Dawn blew her nose loudly.

"Those creeps!" shouted Terri, gritting her teeth.

"Shhh! You'll wake everyone!" warned Monique.

"I never want to go back in there. I'm staying with you guys," said Dawn, wiping her nose determinedly. "I don't care what the director says. If he won't let me stay here, I'm catching the next bus home!"

"Okay, okay," said Angela, leading the way to her bunk. "Come on. We'll figure it all out in the morning."

"Yeah, let's get some sleep," said Sonya.

"I'll never stop itching," Dawn mumbled.

Dawn climbed into Angela's bed and fell asleep right away.

Sonya lay awake for a long time, worrying. Camp was supposed to have been a romantic dream, but it was turning into a horrible nightmare instead.

Chapter Five

"I'm never going back!" exclaimed Dawn.

"You have to get her out of there!" Monique told Merrie. The girls always went to Merrie even though she wasn't Dawn's counselor because she was the most sympathetic.

Sonya, Dawn, Terri, Angela, and Monique were crowded around Merrie outside Cabin 4 the next morning.

"I'll never get any sleep!" exclaimed Dawn tearfully, scratching her leg.

"How could anybody sleep with spiders all over them?" Sonya asked.

"I have the bites to prove it, too. You want to see?" Dawn lifted the leg of her cutoffs to show Merrie.

"Look, I promise I'll get you out of there and put you in Cabin Four with your friends, Dawn," said Merrie. "I'll convince the director to put a foldout bed in there or something. But first you'd better go to the infirmary to see about those spider bites."

"Oh, thank you, Merrie!" cried Dawn, flinging her arms around the counselor.

"You're welcome," said Merrie, shaking her head. "I'm sorry this had to happen."

"Me, too," said Dawn. After Merrie was gone and they were walking to the infirmary, she told the others, "You know, I'm almost grateful to those spiders."

Sonya laughed. "Yeah, if it weren't for them, you'd still be in Cabin Five."

After the nurse had put salve on Dawn's bites, the girls went to sign up for another contest in their war against Camp Honeywell.

"Let's enter the costume war," suggested Angela. "I know we can win that one."

"Yeah. Sonya can sew, and besides, we're on a winning streak," said Terri. All the girls had easily put away their tennis sets.

"It's bad luck to talk like that," warned Dawn.

"Don't worry," said Sonya, putting their names under Costume Making. "At least I know Howard can't sew."

They trooped into the arts and crafts cabin to see what supplies were available. A sign saying "Costume Materials" was set up on one of the long tables. It was covered with bolts of fabric, leather, beads, feathers, needles, and thread in all colors. Some girls were already working.

"Oooh! This is perfect!" cried Dawn, unrolling a bolt of bright purple fabric.

"Let's make saris, those Indian wraparound dresses," suggested Angela as she pulled a bolt of see-through fabric from the pile.

"Great idea!" exclaimed Sonya. "That way we don't have to do too much sewing."

"I'm not wearing a dress," grumbled Terri.

"Come on, Terri," pleaded Angela.

"If Terri's not wearing a dress, I'm not wearing one," Monique declared.

"Monique, do you have to do everything Terri does?" asked Sonya.

"No, I don't," Monique said, sticking her hands on her hips and pouting. "I just don't like dresses, either."

"Okay, let's make something else for them," suggested Dawn. "I hate arguing."

There was a big roll of plastic in one corner. Sonya had an idea. "I know. We can make you something out of this. You can be Martians."

"Hey, good thinking," said Monique. She dragged the huge roll over to the table.

Sonya took the girls' measurements with a tape measure and cut out pants for each of them. Then she had them sew them up with big hand stitches.

Meanwhile, Dawn had wrapped herself in the gauzy sheer fabric, and Angela cut off the excess.

Sonya showed them how to tuck in the ragged edge of the fabric so that it didn't show on the outside.

Dawn checked her reflection in a full-length mirror. "Hey, I look like a real Indian."

"Except for your blond hair."

"I know! We'll cover our hair with shawls made from the same fabric," said Sonya.

Excitedly she started the girls making shawls. They were able to wear all their costumes over their clothes. Terri's and Monique's clothes showed through their plastic outfits and made them look even more like aliens.

Dawn dug into a huge box that contained hats and scarves. "Look what I found!" she cried, holding up two sparkly headbands with bobbing antennae sticking out of them.

"Oh, great!" Monique stuck a headband over her frizzy hair. "Take me to your leader."

"Outer space, here we come!" Terri put on a headband, then zoomed around the crafts cabin with her arms outstretched.

"Okay, okay. Let's get going," said Sonya. "We have to get ready to go to swimming and then we can dress for the contest."

After swimming Sonya and her friends ran all the way back to their cabin to change into their costumes. On the way they passed lots of other girls dressed in wonderfully strange outfits. There was a fly, a refrigerator, cartoon characters, and a cat chasing a mouse.

"Everybody had such good ideas!" exclaimed Dawn.

"Well, so do we," said Sonya. "Long River stands a really good chance of winning."

They stepped out of their swimsuits and left them in wet heaps on the floor before they put on their saris and space suits. Sonya went around to each girl and made up her face.

"We really look great," said Monique, grinning at herself in the mirror.

"Come on. Let's get out to the contest," said Terri, banging open the door. "It starts in five minutes."

The girls charged across the camp to the dining hall, where both boy and girl contestants were already gathered. Sonya gazed around the room at the costumes and still felt confident about theirs. There were some bird costumes, a group of girls dressed as flowers, and some boys dressed as vegetables.

The judges were four of the counselors, two from each camp. They moved around the room, busily taking notes on each of the costumes. After about half an hour, they dismissed everyone.

"The results will be posted on the bulletin board by dinnertime," called one of the counselors.

"I can't stand the suspense," said Terri. "Let's go play baseball."

"Like this?" cried Dawn.

"Of course not. You can't move in that dumb dress," said Terri.

Once they were back in their cabin, the girls took

turns unwrapping one another from the saris and help-
ing Terri and Monique out of their space suits.

When it was time for dinner, all the Camp Long
River costume contestants ran to the bulletin board
to check on the contest results.

Sonya stared at the piece of paper in disbelief. The
winners of the contest were boys—Maurice Bick-
worth and his team.

Sonya's friends crowded around her, almost smash-
ing her against the bulletin board.

"*Boys* won the costume contest? I can't believe
it!" exclaimed Dawn, slumping down on the ground.

"It's not fair. I was sure we'd win," said Monique.

"What do boys know about costumes?" scoffed
Terri, stamping her feet.

"They know all about costume design," said a
boy's voice from behind them.

Sonya whirled around to stare into a pair of steady
blue eyes. The boy they belonged to was still wearing
his costume—a tomato costume made from fabric
stretched over a wire frame.

"I'm Maurice," he said, grinning. Behind him were
four other boys, a giggling carrot, a potato, a celery
stalk, and a cucumber.

Sonya wondered how come she hadn't noticed
them before. They must have been in a far corner.

"You made that costume?" Sonya asked, studying
Maurice. She had to admit that his costume was sen-
sational. It really was like a tomato.

"And all the other vegetables," said Maurice
proudly.

"If I didn't know tomatoes don't grow that big, I'd think you were a real one," said Dawn.

Maurice laughed. "That was the general idea. My father designs costumes for the theater."

"Lucky you," said Angela. "What theater?"

"Off-Broadway theaters," replied Maurice.

Angela gasped. "Wow, did you hear that, guys?" She was very impressed by anyone who worked professionally in the theater.

"So this means that all the girls have cleanup duty tonight," Maurice went on.

"Oh, no big deal," said Monique.

"Yeah, it'll be easy," said Sonya.

The other vegetables laughed, causing their leafy tops to flop over their eyes.

"See you, Maurice," said Angela, waggling her fingers at him before she turned around to join her friends. They walked toward the arts and crafts cabin. "Wow, a celebrity."

Sonya opened the door of the cabin and gasped. Her friends peered over her shoulder.

"Oh, no!"

"Those creeps!"

The cabin looked as if it had been the scene of a real war. Powdered paints were spilled on the floor, candy bar wrappers and soda cans were everywhere, and bolts of fabric were unrolled around the room. The jars of beads and buttons had been emptied onto the tables, and thread was all tangled up.

"This is going to take us *days* to clean up!" cried

Sonya through gritted teeth. "Even with all the other girl contestants working."

"We shouldn't have to clean this up," said Angela, picking up a skein of tangled yarn.

"Yeah, the boys made this mess—they should do it," Monique said, kicking a soda can across the room.

"I guess that's why they call these contests 'wars,' said Sonya.

Terri looked as if she was ready to explode as she yelled, "Okay, guys, this really does mean *war!*"

Chapter Six

✿

Early the next morning Sonya was in the paddock, practicing dressage, or precision movements, with a horse named Mickey. Sonya and Mickey had taken to each other almost instantly, and the two worked well together. Sonya would give the signals to turn or back up.

She was concentrating so hard that she wasn't prepared when Mickey whinnied and started to trot. Sonya lost her balance for a second and had to tighten up on the reins to control the big bay horse.

"Whoa!" she cried, pulling up on the reins.

"Whoa!" another voice called.

Mickey was stopped, and Sonya turned around to focus on Howard, who was sitting on the fence, grinning.

"You spooked my horse," she said angrily. "All you ever do is cause trouble!"

Sonya clicked her tongue to give Mickey the signal

to move off toward the far side of the ring and away from Howard.

"Hey, Sonya, wait!" cried Howard, running beside the fence. "I didn't mean to spook your horse."

"What did you mean to do?" she demanded, glaring at him.

"I just wanted to watch you practice," he explained, hooking his legs around the fence slats as he boosted himself on the rail. "I wish I could ride a horse like that."

"Well, it takes practice, like anything else," she said, stroking Mickey's neck. He tossed his head and whinnied to show he liked the attention.

"Do you think you could show me how?" he asked.

"I doubt it. You'd probably fall off," she said meanly.

"Sonya, look, I'm sorry for how I've been acting lately," he said.

"You're not sorry. You just want me to show you how to ride better," she said.

"No, I am really sorry," he answered in a small voice.

As she stared down at him, she realized how much she had missed him. He seemed so small and sad sitting there on the fence. Howard was usually cheerful, and she hated to see him like this.

"Oh, okay," she replied. "Come on over here, and I'll try to give a few pointers."

She swung her leg up and slid down off Mickey. Then she gave Howard a leg up onto the horse after asking her riding instructor if she could give Howard a lesson.

"Okay. Just sit quietly on the horse to get a feel for him—don't move. Just try to find that point at which you and he connect."

Sonya handed Mickey's reins over to Howard and patted the horse's neck. Howard did as he was told. "Very good. Just stay that way until you feel really comfortable, then walk slowly around the ring, controlling him only with your legs."

After a few minutes Howard was doing it perfectly. He grinned like a maniac. "Wow, look at me."

"Great. Okay, now you're going to get the horse to back up. Lightly flick him on the leg you want him to start out on. Turn slightly in your seat so he knows to move backward."

Howard followed the instructions, and after three or four attempts Mickey backed up.

"See? You did it."

He was beaming from ear to ear. "I can't believe it. I actually controlled the horse."

"Sure."

"This is the most fun I've had at camp so far," he declared, blushing, as he looked at her.

"Oh, yeah?" She felt suddenly hopeful. Maybe it wasn't going to be the worst summer ever.

"Yeah." Howard raised his eyes and his face turned even brighter red. "I want to get off now."

"Why? I thought this was the most fun you've had yet," she said, frowning.

"No, well—yeah, it is, b-but—" he stammered.

The horse flicked his ears back and forth. Howard slid off and ran to the fence, then continued running until he was out of sight behind a stable.

"Howard!" she yelled. Then she saw a gang of boys, headed by Robbie, moving straight toward her. They were the reason Howard had taken off.

"Hey, that was Howard Tarter Sauce!" cried Robbie, running after him.

Sonya saw Howard sprint away toward a trail and disappear down it. The boys were still searching for him around the barn.

Disappointed, Sonya climbed back on Mickey.

"The boys are definitely out to get us," declared Terri as she furiously swept powdered paint off the floor of the crafts cabin. The girls hadn't had time to clean up the mess the day before. "They told their counselors we made all this mess."

"No way!" cried Monique.

Just then a group of girls, headed by Lauren, clustered in the doorway. None of them had been in the costume war. "What's going on?" asked Lauren.

"Ew!" One girl picked a squashed, half-eaten sandwich off the floor.

"Yeah, why'd you trash this room?" asked a girl named Shelley Zeck.

"We didn't!" exclaimed Sonya. "It was the boys! They declared this cabin a disaster area so nobody can do crafts today."

"And I guess all the counselors believe the boys'

story, because the girls have to clean it up," Terri went on.

Lauren leered at them all. "Let us know when it's safe to enter."

The girls giggled and stalked off.

Terri clenched her fists. "We have to fight back."

"We do?" asked Sonya.

"Of course. You want to just sit here and let the boys walk all over us?" Terri demanded, flinging a cloud of blue powder in the air and covering three other girls with the paint.

Sonya's spirits sank. She was just about to tell her friends about her morning with Howard, but now she wouldn't.

Dawn was rewinding the skeins of yarn with Nell O'Dea. "But how? Put spiders in their beds?"

Angela giggled. "Great idea."

"Just what they deserve," said Monique from her station at the sink, washing paintbrushes.

"I think when it's their turn to clean up, we should make the job messier than they made ours," suggested Terri.

"I don't think that's possible," said Sonya. She was carefully rolling up bolts of material with one of the other girls, Lizzie Manning. "Nobody could make a bigger mess than this."

"You haven't seen anything yet," said Terri, rubbing her paint-stained hands together.

"We'll pick a contest that's a sure winner for us," said Monique as she picked up basket weavers.

"The bake-off contest!" cried Dawn, dropping one

of the balls of yarn onto the floor straight into a pile of glitter.

"Perfect," said Angela.

"And we'll make that big kitchen the messiest place you've ever seen!" said Terri.

"Are you sure you want to do this?" asked Sonya.

"Well, yeah. Why not?" asked Terri.

"Well, I mean, I'll bet they'll do it back to us when they win again," said Sonya. "This might not prove to be very much fun."

"They might not ever win another war," said Terri, beaming at her friends.

"Yeah, not if we have anything to say about it," said Monique. And all the girls cheered and whooped.

Sonya felt outnumbered and worried. The morning at the stables with Howard was the best time she'd had since she had come to camp. She didn't want to spoil things by having a big war over messes.

But what choice did she have? Worse, with baking experts like Dawn and Angela on their side, she was sure the girls had to *win* the bake-off!

Chapter Seven

"Look, they don't even know how to use an electric mixer," Angela whispered to Sonya.

She pointed at the boys, who were working at the far end of the kitchen with one of the mixers. Sonya and her friends were the only ones to enter this war and were baking cakes and cupcakes that would be judged after dinner that night. Sonya had wanted to use her recipes for Super Delicious Chocolate Fudge Cake and her Candy Bar Pie, but Angela insisted they use some of her mom's prizewinning recipes.

"Shouldn't we help them?" Sonya asked, watching Robbie trying to figure out what attachments to use on the big industrial mixer.

"Let them figure it out themselves," said Terri.

Dawn expertly measured out flour for the cakes into a huge mixing bowl. Suddenly she jumped back a foot, screaming.

"What's wrong?" asked Sonya, coming to her side.

Everyone stopped what they were doing and crowded around Dawn.

"Weevils! In the flour! Look at them wiggling all over the place!" cried Dawn. Little bugs crawled across the flour. The flour drifted from the measuring cup to the floor like light snow.

"Gross!" cried Sonya. "What do we do?"

"Throw out the whole bag of flour," said Angela knowledgeably. "Unless you like bugs cooked in your food."

"Oh, no!" Dawn dumped the bag of flour in a big garbage bag and closed it with a wire twistie.

The boys were watching them, laughing hysterically.

"I wish they'd shut up," said Monique, scowling at the boys. "They sound like a bunch of hyenas."

"We have to ask them for some flour if we want to finish our cakes," said Sonya.

"This stinks," said Terri.

Sonya walked over and smiled at Robbie. "Can we borrow some flour, please?"

Robbie grinned at her. "Sure. Why not? We're going to win anyway."

"We should make them bake with buggy flour," suggested Maurice. "Then they couldn't win."

Howard caught Sonya's eye and instantly turned away.

"They can't win," said Robbie, handing Sonya a huge sack of flour. Terri ran over to help her carry it back.

Meanwhile, Angela was trying to get the electric

mixer to work. "The blades are all bent," she said, trying to unbend them.

"Somebody must have tried to mix a hippopotamus with this mixer," said Dawn, staring at the bent blades.

"We have all the luck," said Sonya. "We still have hands, so let's get to work."

Everyone groaned as they took turns mixing the heavy batter with big wooden spoons.

"Look at it this way. It's a good workout," said Monique.

"I'd rather be doing gymnastics," said Terri.

Finally the batter was ready to go into the oven. Sonya saw Howard taking a cake out of their oven. "Look! They're way ahead of us!"

"As long as the cakes are baked by tonight, we're okay," said Angela, putting the cake pans in the oven.

She turned the dial to the correct temperature and set the timer. While the cakes were baking, the girls worked on the cupcake batter.

About fifteen minutes later Sonya was spooning cupcake batter into little paper cups when she smelled something burning.

"What's burning?" she asked.

"Must be the boys' cakes!" cried Angela excitedly.

"Yeah, they must've forgotten to set their timer," said Dawn.

"Check your cakes!" yelled Monique.

Worriedly, Howard peered in the oven. He looked over at Sonya. "Ours are fine."

Sonya exchanged a panicked glance with each of her friends. They all had the same thought at the same time and rushed to their oven. Sonya flung the door open and smoke poured out, causing her to double over in a sudden coughing fit.

"Oh, no! Our cakes! What happened?" cried Dawn, grabbing pot holders and pulling the cakes out.

In the background Sonya could hear the boys laughing again. She stared down at the blackened dough crusted in the cake pan.

"Why did our stuff burn? It was only in for fifteen minutes, and it was supposed to cook for an hour!" she cried, waving away the smoke with a tea towel.

Angela was examining the dial on the oven. "This is why. The dial got turned all the way up to Broil."

Terri glared over at the boys. "I'm sure they did it on purpose so our stuff would burn."

"We would have seen them, Terri," said Sonya. "One of us could have done it accidentally."

"But not everybody wants us to mess up like the boys do," insisted Terri.

"It's too late to worry how it happened now," Angela told her.

"I've never had a broiled cake before," said Monique, staring at the black gunky mess.

"Taste," said Terri, stabbing a knife into the hardening blob. "It should be great," she added sarcastically.

"A first-prize cake," said Sonya, slumping against the stainless steel counter.

"Well, we just have to start over," said Dawn.

Reluctantly the girls measured out more ingredients for more cakes. Angela carefully set the oven dial on 350°. Sonya gazed longingly at the boys, who were already decorating their beautiful cakes with colorful pieces of candy.

"Okay, here we go again," said Sonya, pouring batter into the clean cake pans.

"Are you sure the oven's set right, Angie?" asked Terri.

"Yeah. Right on." Angela smiled confidently.

"Did you remember all the ingredients?" asked Dawn.

"Yeah, we got them all."

"You got the chocolate in the chocolate cake and the bananas in the banana-nut cake?" asked Monique, giggling.

"It's not funny. Yes, we did," said Sonya, sniffing both cakes.

"Ready, set, *Go!*" yelled Terri, shoving the cake pans into the oven.

Sonya saw the boys leaving the kitchen. Their cakes were set on one of the big stainless steel tables, one of them beautifully decorated with thin swirls and curls of chocolate. They had also made a pie.

"They sure make nice-looking cakes and pies," said Dawn.

"Yeah, but how do they taste? That's the big test," replied Sonya. The boys' pie looked oddly familiar to her.

Angela checked the cakes every five minutes to see if they were okay. Finally when they were done, she carefully pulled them out of the oven and slid them onto the counter.

"They're crooked," said Dawn.

"They're slanted," said Terri.

"They look like ski slopes without snow," noted Sonya.

"What're we going to do?" asked Angela, flinging her hands in the air. "This is awful!"

"We can decorate them to look like ski slopes," suggested Dawn. "We'll make white frosting."

"But nobody will know they're supposed to be slopes. They'll just look like snowy mountains," Sonya pointed out.

Dawn rummaged around in drawers. She held up toothpicks, and some Christmas cake decorations. "We'll use these little plastic people as skiers and the toothpicks as skis and poles," she said.

"Brilliant," said Monique.

Decorating the cakes was actually the most fun part of the contest, Sonya thought as she used icing to glue the little skiers on their toothpick skis.

"These cakes are so original, I'm sure we'll win," said Terri. She had made a ski ramp out of a piece of cardboard.

"Let's keep our fingers crossed," said Dawn, crossing all of her fingers except her thumbs.

Sonya and her friends sat at the table in the dining room after dinner, waiting for the results of the baking contest.

The cakes were displayed on a table covered with decorated butcher paper.

"Our cakes don't look normal," said Sonya, watching Merrie and the other judges checking out the display.

Lauren sidled up to Dawn. "Nobody would bake cakes that look like that on purpose."

"Why not?" asked Dawn. "Other people just aren't as creative as us."

"Yeah," agreed Angela.

But Sonya started to worry. She went over to look at the cakes again. Howard's cake was entitled Super Delicious Chocolate Double Fudge Cake and the pie was called Candy Bar Pie.

"Those are *my* recipes!" cried Sonya in horror. She'd given him her best recipes on the day they'd gone to the movies together—because he liked them so much!

Lauren laughed out loud. "Looks like you've been had," she said.

"Go away," said Dawn, sticking close to Sonya.

"Yeah, split, will you?" Terri said to her.

But Lauren hung around.

"Attention, campers!" cried Merrie. "We're going to announce the winners of the Bake-Off. The winners are—"

One of the other counselors, Geraldine, shouted out, *"Ta daaaa!"* and everyone stared at Merrie expectantly.

"The boys' team, with cake recipes by Howard Tarter!" announced Merrie, applauding.

The boys cheered and whooped wildly.

"My cakes!" cried Sonya in horror.

"Your cakes?" quizzed Lauren. "Not anymore."

Miserable, Sonya watched Howard and the other boys strut up to Merrie and bow wildly.

Lauren nudged Sonya in the ribs. "Hey, don't be such a sore loser."

Sonya and her friends glared at her.

"Yeah, sure. We should be thrilled, right?" said Terri.

"I can't believe it!" exclaimed Dawn. "Here I am, a baker's daughter, and I can't even win a *baking contest!"*

"Yeah, me, too," said Angela. "I'm an expert on good food."

"Between the two of us we should've been able to win any cooking contest," said Dawn.

Sonya tapped herself on the chest. "Guys, those were *my* recipes. He used *my* recipes, can you believe that?"

"What a slime!" said Terri, clenching her fists.

Sonya crossed her arms over her chest. "One thing's for sure. I'm not going to feel sorry for Howard—ever again!"

Chapter Eight

❀

"Oh, no!" cried Sonya.

"Barf!" exclaimed Terri.

"What do we do now?" cried Monique, stomping into the kitchen.

"It looks like it was hit by an earthquake," said Dawn.

The kitchen was covered with a fine layer of flour. There was a pile of sugar on the floor, and eggs had been broken and dried on the countertops. When Sonya opened the refrigerator door, raisins and chocolate chips spilled out onto the linoleum.

"This is the worst mess yet!" she exclaimed.

"It's our own fault," reminded Angela. "We thought we were going to win and they'd clean up."

"But I think they came back and *added* to it!" exclaimed Terri.

"It just looks different when you have to clean it up yourself," said Sonya.

"It's bad enough they had to win the Bake-Off, but

57

for us to have to clean this up as well is lousy,'' said Angela, shaking out a dirty tea towel.

"I vote that we don't do it,'' announced Terri. "Leave it for the boys.''

"Great idea!'' cried Sonya.

"Can we get away with that?'' asked Dawn worriedly. "I mean, we did make most of the mess, and we are supposed to clean up if we lose.''

"Let's ask a counselor,'' said Terri. "We'll tell them the boys did it on purpose.''

Sonya pulled some empty packages out of the garbage and dumped them on the counter. "Wait till Howard finds out he has to clean up this mess!''

"Yeah. That'll teach him for stealing your recipes!'' cried Dawn loyally.

The girls marched out of the kitchen and back into the dining hall in search of a counselor. They found Merrie first, pulling on a sweater, getting ready to go out to the campfire.

"Hi, girls. What's up? Uh-oh, you look like you're on the warpath,'' she said, eyeing their matched, angry expressions.

"It's those boys again,'' Sonya began. "They purposely messed up the kitchen—just so we'd have a horrible mess to clean up!''

Merrie sighed and pushed her fingers through her long blond hair. "Look, girls. I'm sorry about that. You lost the contest, so y'all are responsible for the cleanup.''

"No way!'' declared Terri, stomping her feet.

Sonya put a hand on Terri's arm. "Terri, don't.''

Since they had tried to trick the boys with the cleanup, she didn't think Terri should protest too much.

"I know it doesn't seem fair, but that's the way it is," said Merrie. "I'll see what I can do for the future, though."

Sonya swallowed hard as they walked back to the kitchen. When they got there, the boys were waiting at the door.

Howard grinned at Sonya.

Just the sight of him made her furious. "What are you doing here?" she demanded, barging right past him into the kitchen.

"We came to watch," he replied.

"We didn't have anything else to do," said another boy.

"I always knew a girl's place was in the kitchen," said Robbie, guffawing loudly.

Howard and the other boys laughed.

"You idiot!" Sonya grabbed the first thing she could reach—a sack of flour. She dumped the whole thing on Howard's head.

Everyone gasped, then laughed.

"Hey, Howie, you look like the Pillsbury Dough-boy," Robbie commented.

Howard wiped flour out of his eyes, walked over to Sonya, and shook flour on her. Then he squirted a packet of liquid chocolate onto the front of her shirt.

Terri, Dawn, Angela, and Monique flew into action, flinging a couple of eggs at the boys.

"Hey no fair!" yelled Howard.

"They're out to get us!" cried another boy, shielding himself with his arms.

"Run!" yelled Maurice, taking off at top speed.

"Get out of here!" shouted Terri, charging after them with an egg. She threw it at Robbie and hit him in the back.

Raw egg and shell oozed down the back of Robbie's T-shirt.

Sonya, Dawn, Terri, Angela, and Monique charged the boys with baking powder. Sonya grabbed one by the shirt and squashed a stick of margarine into the back of his hair. Dawn grabbed a can of whipping cream and blasted Howard. He pelted her with chocolate chips, then ran, with little clouds of cream flying off his clothes.

The boys laughed and ran out into the night, disappearing down a dark trail.

"They're gone," said Sonya, wiping her slimy hands on her jeans.

"Yeah, but we still have to clean up," Monique pointed out. Margarine wrappers, chocolate chips, and flour sacks were globbed together on the floor.

"And we have more of a mess to clean up now," said Dawn.

"Also, this is going to cost us our allowances for the next two weeks," Angela reminded them. They all looked gloomy as it dawned on them that they'd have to pay for all the wasted food.

"But right now we need mops and sponges, wherever they are," Terri said.

They scrambled around, picking up what they could by hand. Then they started mopping up the sludgy floor.

They cleaned for what seemed like days and finished at about ten o'clock.

"We didn't sign up for another war for tomorrow," said Sonya sleepily.

"I don't want to enter any more wars," said Dawn.

"We've got to enter at least one more, one we think we can win—" said Sonya.

"That worked so well the last time," added Angela.

"But this time we'll be positive," insisted Sonya. "And then, when they lose, we'll make an even bigger mess for them to clean up."

"But we won't make any mess until we're sure we've won," suggested Monique. "I don't want to go through this again."

"Yeah. Let's not get caught in our own trap anymore," added Angela.

Wearily Sonya and her friends trudged over to the dining hall to check out the war activities for the next day.

"There's only one thing that isn't filled up—the wilderness trip," said Angela miserably. "I hate hiking."

"Not only that, look at the time," noted Dawn. "We have to be up at five in the morning to go on the hike."

"I'm ready to drop right now," said Sonya, moaning.

"Maybe we shouldn't enter," suggested Angela.

"Well, Monique and I are great hikers," said Terri.

"But all of us are going to be exhausted," Angela pointed out. "We're already exhausted."

"Yeah. How are we going to win a wilderness hike contest when we can't even keep our eyes open?" asked Sonya.

Chapter Nine

"Got everything?" asked Sonya. She was surrounded by her best friends at the foot of the mountain they planned to hike. Everybody was dressed in jeans and hiking boots. They had packs on their backs and canteens slung around their shoulders.

"Compass!" cried Monique, prying the compass out of her pocket.

"Food!" exclaimed Angela, tapping her pack.

"Seems like we've got everything," said Sonya.

"Wait a minute!" shouted Merrie, clumping up to the girls in her heavy hiking boots. Lauren Tompkins was running to keep up with her. "We have too many girls in one of the other groups, so y'all have one more person. You know Lauren?"

"Hi," said Lauren, pulling on a short piece of her red hair.

A little gasp escaped from Dawn's lips. Everyone turned to stare at her. She had turned pale.

Lauren smiled. Sonya swallowed hard. Not only

were they all exhausted, but they had to put up with snotty Lauren as well.

"Have you got everything, Lauren?" asked Sonya. Maybe if she started out being nice to the girl, everything would be okay.

"Yeah. Do you have enough food for me?" Lauren asked.

"There's extra stuff in my pack," said Angela.

"Okay, then I guess we're ready," said Sonya, unfolding a big map. The girls crowded around to get a look. She traced her finger along the route. "We just go up the mountain like this, following the blue trail markers, and come down this other trail. It's simple."

"Up and down," said Terri, in case there was doubt in anyone's mind.

"Yeah, I figured that out," said Lauren. "What goes up must come down."

Merrie clapped her hands and called the two groups to order. There were only two groups of girls going.

"Okay, the first group to arrive back here is the winner. Ann Ritter, your counselor, will be on the trail, keeping an eye out for you. If one of the girls' groups wins, then the boys must clean up all the camp equipment and do laundry. So keep that in mind—Camp Long River *must* win!"

Terri let out a whoop and the other girls followed her example.

Just then Sonya noticed Howard with a group of boys. He had a backpack hoisted onto his skinny back, which made him look like an overburdened tortoise. Boys were patting him on the back and laughing.

"It looks like Howard's made friends finally," said Dawn, who was standing next to Sonya.

"Yeah," said Sonya glumly. "You know, I think I liked it better when they called him a nerd."

"I'll bet they like him because he helped them win the Bake-Off," suggested Angela. "Now he's one of the gang."

"But he cheated," cried Sonya.

Terri shook her head. "Not really cheated. But if it hadn't been for you, he probably would've made something really dumb, like cake mix cupcakes or something."

"He's not that dumb, Terri," said Sonya, feeling a twinge of loyalty for Howard. "I'm sure he would've made something good."

"You'll never know," said Terri, stomping ahead of the others.

Lauren walked over to the girls. "Isn't that the boy who used those great recipes for the Bake-Off?" she asked, pointing to Howard.

Sonya glowered. "Yes, and they were my recipes."

"Oh, sure," said Lauren sarcastically. "So you let him win?"

"No! It's a long story," said Sonya, marching ahead. "Okay, everyone, let's get going!"

Reluctantly Angela got to her feet and followed her friends. Dawn almost had to run to keep up with the others. Ann, a counselor, was about ten minutes ahead of the girls.

"Oh, look, a deer!" cried Monique. She stopped to take a picture, but the big buck vanished into the brush.

"Wow, they're fast," said Terri. "I wish I could be that fast."

After they had been walking for fifteen minutes, Lauren sighed heavily. "Can we stop and rest now?"

"No!" exclaimed Terri. "We haven't gone far enough."

Sonya was hoping to catch sight of Howard, but she knew he and his group were on the other side of the mountain.

Angela began handing out dried fruit and nuts.

"Angie, we're not hungry yet!" cried Sonya.

"But this keeps our mouths occupied so we don't get bored," Angela explained.

"We could talk," said Monique.

"Then we run out of breath," said Lauren, huffing and puffing beside her.

"Yeah. Don't you have anything that's not so healthy?" asked Monique, peering into the unzipped pocket of Angela's pack.

"Chocolate bars. But they're for later," said Angela. "We should save them for last."

"Something to look forward to if we live through this awful hike," said Lauren, picking prickles out of her pants.

"You act as if we're climbing Mount Everest," said Terri. "Now, come on."

Everyone was quiet for a while. They hiked for an hour and a half, then a loud, shrill scream pierced the air.

They all turned to see where the scream was coming from. Dawn was way down the trail, hopping from one foot to the other, flapping her arms in the air.

"Bees!" cried Lauren, screaming and taking off up the trail and away from Dawn.

Sonya and Angela rushed to Dawn's rescue. "Oh, no, she stepped on a wasps' nest! They're all over!"

"Stand still!" ordered Terri.

"No, get out of their way, Dawn. They're already mad!" cried Angela, batting the wasps off herself and Sonya.

Sonya and Angela half carried Dawn up the trail, out of the range of the wasps. Some of them were still clinging to Dawn's clothing.

"Get them off me!" cried Dawn, swatting them with a folded map. Finally they flew away.

Sonya knelt to examine the wasp stings all over Dawn's legs. "They really got you."

"Are you allergic to wasp stings?" asked Monique.

"I don't think so," said Dawn.

"Who has the first-aid kit?" asked Sonya.

"I do," said Monique. She dropped her pack on the ground and dug in it for the kit. She put some salve on the bites.

"Wow, they stung you right through your socks," said Angela, peeling down Dawn's socks.

"They're awful," said Dawn, tears drying on her smudged cheeks.

"Well, you'd probably act like that if someone stepped on your house," Sonya said.

"I can't stand nature," declared Lauren. "Something bad always happens outdoors."

"That's not true," insisted Dawn. "Some good things happen, too."

"Like what?" asked Lauren.

"Well, you could find a rare butterfly," said Dawn weakly.

"With my luck I'd fall in a bunch of poison oak," said Lauren.

"Do you think you can walk, Dawn?" asked Sonya.

"Yeah, I think so," said Dawn. She hooked her arms around Sonya's and Angela's shoulders. "I feel okay."

She limped along the trail slowly.

Terri watched her, shaking her head. "Maybe we should just go back down. There's no way we're going to win this hike with Dawn hopping like that."

"I'll hop fast," said Dawn, demonstrating. She lost her balance and had to reach for a tree trunk.

"Maybe we should leave you here," suggested Lauren.

The other girls turned as one and glared at her.

"So I can be eaten by a bear?" asked Dawn.

"Come on. Just go slowly. If you think you need to turn back, let us know," said Sonya, taking Dawn's arm.

They walked farther up the trail. It narrowed and became rockier and steeper, so the girls had to use their hands to hold on for part of the way. Finally the trail leveled out and they were walking beside a stream.

"Wow, look. A deer," said Monique, pointing out a deer that had come to the stream to drink.

Sonya put her hand on Monique's arm. "Don't scare it away. It's so beautiful."

Angela quietly sat down on a big rock and set her backpack down on the ground beside her. "Whew! He's gone. Let's eat."

"No. Let's go downstream a little farther," insisted Terri.

The others trudged along behind her reluctantly. She led the way across the swollen stream, crossing on rocks. The girls followed her example.

"Help!" cried Angela. She was the last to cross.

Sonya turned around to see Angela lying in the stream on her back with her legs in the air, clutching on to a rock to keep herself from being dragged downstream. Quickly Sonya sloshed through the water and grabbed Angela under the armpits.

"Just get to your feet and you'll be fine," she said. Terri grabbed Angela's other side, and they pulled her to her feet.

"Thanks," said a sopping, soggy Angela.

"Now can we have lunch?" whined Lauren.

Dawn went right up to Lauren's face and said, "Don't you care about anybody? What's wrong with you? One of my best friends just nearly *drowned!*"

"Yeah! How'd you like that to happen to you?" demanded Terri, glaring at Lauren.

"Okay, okay. I'm just hungry, that's all," she said, grumbling.

Angela's face went suddenly white. "Oh, no. The lunch. Where's the lunch?"

Sonya and the others turned to search for Angela's bright red pack but didn't see it anywhere.

"Well, you were wearing it, weren't you?" asked Lauren.

"I had it half off, because I thought I could balance better—" Her expression darkened. "Oh, no! It's probably in the river!"

The girls looked downstream. There was a froth of water down near some rapids, but no backpack.

"I see it!" cried Dawn, hobbling along the edge of the stream.

"Be careful!" yelled Angela. Everyone ran after Dawn. In the far distance they could see the pack bobbing its way downstream. They ran down the side of the stream for a while, trying to catch up to it, but the water was moving so fast, no one could get the pack.

Finally they went back to Angela, who had put on an extra sweatshirt Sonya had brought. Her teeth were chattering only a little now.

"There went our food supply," said Terri.

"What? We'll *starve!*" exclaimed Lauren indignantly. She had been lying on a big warm rock the whole time. She turned to Angela. "How could you be so stupid?"

"It's easy. Want to try?" Angela grinned into Lauren's smug face. "You just cross the stream like this—"

She demonstrated with her fingers on pebbles.

"Okay, okay. If we can't eat, then let's keep going," said Terri.

"But we'll get weak," said Lauren.

"You can go back if you want," said Angela, dusting herself off.

"Not by myself," Lauren said, crossing her arms over her chest.

"We're not turning back," said Terri.

Everyone was dirty and exhausted, but they all agreed to go on.

"We've got to keep going," said Dawn with determination.

"We've got to beat the boys," Sonya said.

They walked through the squishy mud next to the stream. Then after about an hour of walking along the stream, Sonya noticed something. "You know, I haven't seen any blue trail arrows for a long time."

"Me, neither," said Monique.

They sat down and consulted their map. Sonya saw where the trail went up, away from the stream. They were headed in the wrong direction.

"We should have gone up the hill here, instead of following the stream," she said.

"Oh, no!" cried Monique. "We must have gone at least a half hour out of our way."

"Just what we need," said Angela, groaning. "I wonder if Ann knows we're lost."

"Can't you guys do anything right?" complained Lauren.

"Be quiet, Lauren, or we'll cook you for dinner," said Terri.

"We don't stand a chance of winning," Dawn said glumly.

"Howard knows how to use compasses and maps, so I doubt the boys will get lost," said Sonya.

"The best we can hope for is that one of them will break a leg," said Lauren, trudging along after the others.

Terri turned to her. "Lauren, how'd you ever get to be so much fun to be with?"

Lauren didn't notice Terri was being sarcastic. She shrugged and said, "It comes naturally, I guess."

Sonya took the compass from Monique and checked where they were. If they just traveled back upstream to the fork in the trail, they'd find their way.

The group of girls walked back the way they had come and found the trail, but it was practically overgrown! Sonya looked around for the trail marker, and when she finally found one, it was only a small blue smudge on a tree trunk.

"No wonder! The markers are practically worn off and the trail has hardly been used!" she exclaimed.

"I hope the boys are having the same trouble," said Angela hopefully.

As they walked along the narrow trail, the sky became overcast and the wind began to blow. In the distance thunder rolled.

"Oh, I hope we don't get caught in a storm," said Dawn worriedly.

"It would be just our luck," said Lauren. She started to pop a handful of wild berries into her mouth.

"Don't eat those," warned Sonya. "They could be poisonous."

Lauren dropped the berries to the ground and

stepped on them so they left a deep red stain on the dirt. "I guess I'll just die of malnutrition, then."

"We're almost there," said Terri, peering off into the distance. Below them was a long, blue haze of trees that nearly hid the base camp, which looked like a small brown dot in a clearing.

Everyone grew quiet as they hiked down the mountain. Finally, just as it started to rain, the girls stumbled into base camp, hungry and exhausted.

It was unusually quiet. Sonya cupped her hands around her mouth and yelled, "Hey, anybody here?"

Merrie popped her head around the door of a little, old cabin. "Just me! Hurray, y'all made it! Ann just took a short cut to go looking for you guys."

"Where are the boys?" asked Terri, glancing around.

Merrie grinned. "They're not back yet. You're the first group in. Congratulations! You've won the wilderness hike contest!"

Sonya, Terri, Monique, Dawn, Angela, and Lauren stared at one another in shock.

"We did?"

"Yes. Come on in. I'll bet you're starved."

"Are we ever!" groaned Lauren.

Then the six girls burst into laughter and hugged one another—including Lauren.

Chapter Ten

❀

"Come on, let's go," said Terri, tugging Monique's sweatshirt. "We have to get over to their cabins while they're eating dinner."

"What about *our* dinner?" asked Angela.

"We'll get there late, that's all," explained Terri. She grabbed a bag with all the girls' laundry and slung it over her shoulder.

"Why are you taking our laundry?" asked Dawn.

"For the boys to wash," explained Sonya.

Lauren saw them leaving camp and called out, "Hey, were are you guys going?"

"To Camp Honeywell," called Dawn.

"Want to come?" asked Angela, yawning. Dawn nudged her in the ribs, shaking her head and frowning.

"No, thanks. I'm too tired," Lauren whined.

"We'll go!" cried two enthusiastic girls from the other hiking group, Madeline and Sasha.

They picked up their laundry and hurried to catch up to Terri.

On the way to Camp Honeywell Terri dropped the laundry bag and suddenly dived into the bushes after something.

"Now what's she doing?" Sonya asked.

"Who knows?" said Angela. "All I want to do right now is sleep for three days."

Hugging her sweatshirt, Terri ran back to the others. Something was wriggling inside her shirt. "Look. I found a snake."

Sonya, Dawn, Angela, and Monique took a step backward as the snake's head poked out the top of Terri's sweatshirt.

"Oh, he's cute," said Monique, stepping forward to admire him.

"Are you going to keep him?" asked Sonya worriedly.

"Just what we need, a snake in our cabin," groaned Angela.

"I won't sleep with a snake!" declared Dawn.

"Calm down," said Terri. "He's not going to stay with us."

"Then just what is he going to do?" asked Sonya.

"You'll see," said Terri mysteriously.

They walked down the footpath to Camp Honeywell, with Sonya lugging the laundry bag now. As they approached the camp, they saw boys walking over to their dining hall. The girls made their way stealthily, hiding behind cabins and trees so no one would see them. Each girl kept her eye on Terri's sweatshirt, just in case the snake should suddenly escape.

Sonya sneaked up to the bulletin board outside the dining hall to see where Howard's cabin was located. She also noted that Maurice and Robbie were in the same cabin. Then she hurried back to tell the others.

"Too bad we don't know the other boys' names," said Angela. "We could do a better job."

They found Cabin 6, Howard's cabin, close to the river. All the boys' packs were laid out on the wooden floor of the cabin. Squashed sandwiches, wet socks, dirty shirts, and other unidentifiably gross objects spilled out everywhere.

"Okay, I think we should fill up their packs with wet sand and rocks," said Terri.

"That's mean," said Dawn.

"Not any meaner than what they've done to us," Monique reminded her darkly.

"Yeah, I guess not," Dawn agreed.

"And we can tie their socks together," suggested Sonya.

"Who wants to touch their socks?" asked Angela, making a face.

"I'll do it," Sonya offered. "It's worth it just to know they have to untie a bunch of stinky wet socks."

Madeline and Sasha giggled about everything as they all got to work. Terri lowered the snake into one of the hiking boots and put a book on top of the boot so the snake wouldn't escape.

"I think that's one of Howard's boots," Sonya said.

"How do you know?" asked Sasha.

"Because it's small. Howard's short," explained Sonya.

"Oh, that little kid," said Madeline, giggling again.

Monique and Terri ran back and forth from the creek with handfuls of rocks and sand. Sonya and Madeline worked on the sock project, while Sasha and Angela put rocks on the boys' beds and pulled the blankets over them.

"It will be more fun if they get into bed with the lights out," said Sasha.

"I wish we could be here to watch," Angela said.

Sonya and Madeline tied all the boot- and shoe-laces together, lining the shoes up across the cabin floor. Then they laced all the packs together, too.

"Is there anything else we can do?" asked Sasha, grinning at the mess.

"They'll have to do our laundry," said Terri.

"I can't wait for them to come back and find this mess," said Monique. "They deserve it."

"Come on. We'd better hurry if we want to get any dinner," said Angela.

They left their laundry sack in the cabin and raced back to the dining hall.

As they approached, they could see the lowering sun cast a rosy glow over the lake. Sonya heard the clatter of dishes in the kitchen. Inside the dining hall the kitchen staff were clearing off the long tables.

"Oh, no! We're too late!" exclaimed Dawn, running inside.

"Did you have any food left?" asked Angela.

One of the staff, Bonnie, smiled at them. "Sorry. We have bread and peanut butter, if you're interested."

"Anything!" said Sonya, clutching her stomach.

Bonnie issued them sandwiches and glasses of milk, which they gobbled down quickly. Although they were still slightly hungry, the girls went back to their cabins, knowing they'd sleep well.

"The boys must be trying to get into their beds right now," said Angela sleepily a little later.

"I feel sorry for them," said Dawn sitting on the edge of her bed, and slipping off her fuzzy slippers.

"I don't," Sonya said. She imagined Howard's surprised face as he lay down on a bed of rocks. She smiled as she fell asleep.

The next morning was very hot. The boys marched by the Camp Long River dining hall on the way to their first activity. They all glared at the girls.

"You won't get away with this!" yelled Robbie, raising his fist in the air. Howard looked exhausted.

"Oh, those poor boys," whispered Dawn.

Sonya nudged her in the ribs. "Remember they deserved it."

Later, Sonya and her friends joined Madeline and Sasha at the lake to go swimming. Boring Wanda and Lauren had swimming at the same time, plus a black-haired half-Native American girl from Montana named Nadine, and Sarah from New York.

Sarah was speaking with Sonya after she found out Sonya had spent a couple of years in New York with her father. "When you go to visit him, you should come to visit me, too. We go out to Long Island in the summer, and you could come with us."

"Wow, thanks," said Sonya. She told Sarah about Gladstone, her ranch, and her best friends. "Maybe you can come to Gladstone sometime."

Nadine, who had been listening, butted in just then. "You live on a ranch? Me, too."

"Do you have horses?" asked Monique.

"We raise horses," Nadine explained. She lived far from any town at the foot of the Rocky Mountains.

"I'd love to go there," said Terri. "It sounds so wild and exciting."

"Stop it!" shouted Dawn hysterically.

The girls whirled around to see Lauren dunking poor Dawn in the lake and laughing at her.

Sonya and Monique lunged to Dawn's rescue. Terri swam quickly underwater and popped up right behind Lauren. Sonya grabbed Dawn around the middle and pulled her out of Lauren's reach. Then Terri lifted Lauren, kicking and screaming, out of the lake.

"Put me down *now!*" she squealed, arms and legs sawing the air.

"Not until you promise to leave Dawn alone," Terri said.

"No!"

"Yes!" chorused the other girls.

"I was only playing," grumbled Lauren, pushing strands of sopping red hair out of her eyes.

"You weren't," said Dawn insistently.

"Okay, if you have to be such a baby," sneered Lauren, still trying to wriggle free of Terri.

"Do you promise?" asked Terri again.

"Okay! I promise!" shouted Lauren at the top of her lungs, glaring at Dawn.

A quirky expression came over Terri's face as she suddenly let go of Lauren and watched as she splashed loudly into the water. Everyone watching broke into laughter and clapped as Lauren came up for air.

"I'm going to get you for this, Terri!" she said, narrowing her eyes and shaking a warning finger at her.

"Oh, yeah?" Terri challenged.

"Yeah!"

At dinner that night Nadine, Sarah, Madeline, Sasha, and Wanda all sat at the best friends' table.

"Hey, Wanda's family runs a bakery just like ours," Dawn told everyone. "Isn't that great?"

"Super. Are you going to exchange recipes?" asked Sonya.

"No, but I do want to show you something, Wanda." Dawn left her seat and ran out of the dining room.

A few minutes later she returned with a newspaper clipping to show Wanda. "Hey, guys, I've got to tell you something."

"What, Dawn?" asked Monique.

Just then the counselors called everyone to attention. "We have special after-dinner entertainment for you tonight. The rock band Fried Brains is here to do a few songs after we're all cleaned up."

The room filled with applause and whistles as everyone dashed around putting their plates away and wiping off tables.

After they were seated again, Angela squealed with delight. "I know the drummer. My mother introduced me to her at a party."

"Really? Can I have your autograph?" asked Terri teasingly.

"No, really!" exclaimed Angela, jumping up and down in her seat. She waved at the drummer, a purple-haired girl with dark glasses. "Louise! Louise, it's me, Angie."

"Oh, pul-lease," Terri said, covering her face, embarrassed.

"I think it's great Angie knows the drummer," said Sonya loyally.

"Yeah, me, too," said Monique.

"Who's your mother?" asked Sarah.

"A food writer for *Food Sense* magazine," explained Angela breathlessly.

Fried Brains played several songs, and the campers went wild. After the band finished, the girls crowded around to get their autographs.

"Remember me?" Angela said to the drummer.

Louise squinted at her for a second, then nodded. "Yeah, your mom is that food critic, Ellen King."

Angela beamed with pride. "Yeah."

Finally, when they walked out into the night, they could hear some girls chasing one another around outside their cabin, screeching at the top of their lungs.

It was nearly dark by the time Sonya and her friends went into their cabin.

"Oh, look. Our laundry," said Angela, walking over to the stuffed laundry bag.

A bare lightbulb encircled by moths shone down on the bag.

Angela pulled out a camp T-shirt. "It's turned blue!"

Sonya peered into the bag and moved things around. "Everything's blue!"

"I could kill those boys!" exclaimed Monique.

"And that's not all," Dawn said.

"What?" The girls stared at her in horror.

Dawn took a deep breath. "The boys have stolen all of our underwear."

Chapter Eleven

"It was a dumb idea to let the boys do our laundry," Sonya declared the next morning. She stared at what were once her favorite green- and white-striped shorts, now blue, of course.

"We know that now," said Terri. "But where is our underwear?"

"Yeah?" chimed in Monique. "What would they do with it?"

"Who knows? But I intend to find out," said Sonya.

Even before they had breakfast, the friends trooped over to Camp Honeywell to find Howard and his gang.

Howard was outside his cabin, playing Frisbee with Robbie. Sonya's stomach twisted in a knot at the sight of Robbie. Couldn't Howard find a better friend than him?

Clutching her striped shorts in her fist, Sonya

marched straight up to Howard and caught the oncoming Frisbee in her other hand.

"Nice catch," said Howard, raising his eyebrows in admiration.

"Thanks."

She wasn't expecting any compliments from him. Before she could change her mind about what she was going to say, she blurted out, "What's the meaning of all our clothes being blue?"

Robbie burst into laughter, and Howard looked as if he was trying not to laugh.

"Uh, I guess someone's new blue jeans got in with the other stuff," said Howard. "Sorry."

"Don't you guys know that you're supposed to wash the light stuff separately from the dark stuff?" Sonya demanded.

"Hey, what is this? A laundry lesson?" asked Robbie, socking Howard in the arm playfully.

"You're lucky you got your laundry at all after the way you trashed our cabin," said Howard, balancing the Frisbee on a finger. "We were going to keep it all. This *is* war, after all."

"Which brings us to the next subject," Terri said, storming over to Sonya's side. The other girls followed her and stood close. "Where is our underwear?"

Robbie rolled his eyes and started laughing again. *"Underwear?"*

"It's missing, you dork head," explained Dawn.

Howard shrugged. "We took hostages."

"Whoever heard of hostages in a camp war?" cried Angela.

"You have," said Howard.

"I'm telling our counselor," threatened Monique.

"You'll find out what happened to the underwear soon enough," said Robbie, his face bright red from all the laughing.

"Oh, yeah? You're probably wearing it," accused Terri. Robbie started laughing all over again.

Sonya shook her head angrily. "You haven't been yourself since you got here, Howard. I don't know what happened to you."

"Maybe they give brain transplants at this camp," suggested Angela.

Howard scowled at her. "I'm the same person."

"Maybe," said Sonya. "But you sure seem like a stranger to me. Now I think your stupid friends are right. You are a nerd—just like the other kids say you are!"

Howard's small face turned nearly purple. Robbie jabbed him in the ribs with his elbow.

"Hear that, Howie? I don't think she likes you very much," Robbie said.

"That's probably an understatement," said Angela.

Howard pulled himself up to his full height. "Well, I don't like *you* anymore, either," he said to Sonya.

Sonya couldn't stand to be near him for another minute. She whirled around and stomped off down the trail toward Camp Long River with her friends hurrying right behind her. By the time they arrived back at camp, the other hikers were running around in their pajamas.

"Where's our underwear?"

"Who did the laundry?"

The best friends gathered them all together and explained the situation.

"The boys are holding our underwear hostage," explained Sonya.

One girl turned to another. "Wow. I never expected it to turn into a current event."

"Look!" exclaimed Sonya.

Two girls searching for the underwear had walked out to the camp entrance and found, strung across the Camp Long River sign, a line of girls' blue underwear.

"Everything's blue!" Dawn said as they trooped back to the center of camp with it.

"Whose big idea was it to give those jerks our laundry?" Lauren demanded hotly.

"We were supposed to because they lost, remember?" said Terri.

"You should pay for all our blue underwear," Lauren declared.

"Yeah!" cried Wanda.

"Hey, we're in this stupid mess together," Sonya said.

"Yeah!" agreed Monique.

"But I'm probably the only one here who wears designer underwear," said Lauren emphatically.

"Well, goody for you," said Angela.

"Maybe you can come up with a new fashion statement—true blue underwear, the only kind to wear," quipped Sonya.

Lauren's face turned red. "Okay, I've had it with you guys. I'm going to tell a counselor about this."

Lauren marched off with all the other girls trailing her. Merrie was the first counselor they found, but by the time they found her, she already knew what had happened.

"Okay, we have to talk," she told the two groups of hikers, whose underwear was blue. "Y'all come on into the crafts cabin. They're setting up for breakfast."

Everyone followed her and found a place to sit. Other counselors and campers came in and joined the group.

"Two people just called the camp director and told him about the underwear at the entrance," said Merrie. "This wasn't a very nice thing to do. I know you did it to be funny, but it puts us in a bad light."

"But we didn't do it!" cried Dawn.

"Oh?" asked Merrie.

"The boys did it!"

Merrie frowned. "How did they get all y'all's underwear?"

"We gave it to them," Monique volunteered.

"This is getting stranger by the minute," said Merrie.

"Wait, you don't understand," Sonya said, jumping to her feet. "They had to do our laundry as a part of cleanup, and they turned it all blue and stole our underwear.''

"I get it," said Merrie. Behind her a couple of other counselors smothered giggles. "Obviously, the laundry wasn't a good idea."

"Do you know how weird this sounds?" asked another counselor.

"Yes, but it's true!" exclaimed Angela.

"It's the boys' fault!" yelled Dawn.

"But those dummies gave the boys our laundry," insisted Lauren.

The room grew louder and louder. Merrie consulted with the other counselors.

"*Quiet!*" shouted Merrie at last.

Everyone fell silent.

"Please stay in your cabins except for meals for the rest of the day," she announced. "Or until we get to the bottom of this."

"What a drag," groaned Terri. "There's nothing to do in our cabins."

Just before dinner Howard knocked on the door of Cabin 4. He looked angry and he was clutching a hiking boot to his chest.

"What's up?" asked Terri.

He looked past Terri. "I want to talk to you, Sonya."

"This is a first," said Sonya, sliding off her bunk.

"Come outside," he said.

She glanced around at her friends. "Do you think I need a bodyguard?"

They giggled.

"No, you won't," said Howard. "Just hurry up."

Sonya slipped into her tennis shoes without lacing them and walked outside. Howard placed the boot down on the ground and knelt beside it.

"Why did you put this poor snake in my hiking boot?" he asked.

"I didn't, I m-mean—" she stammered, not wanting to tell him that Terri had been the one to put the snake in there.

"You put a book on top of it, and he could've suffocated," Howard said accusingly.

"I would think he'd die from the smell first," she said, wanting to laugh.

The greeny brown snake poked its head out of the boot, and Howard held it gently. Its little forked tongue flicked in and out of its mouth.

"That's not funny," said Howard. "Sometimes you're the stupidest person I know, Sonya. You don't care about anything that's worth caring about."

Sonya's eyes widened in horror. *"Me?* What about you? What about the way you've been acting toward me? You don't care about anything at all!"

"That's not true. You're wrong," he insisted.

"No, you're wrong," she said. "You're the one who's been pretending we aren't friends. You're the one who's been acting like you're too good for me. So you know what, Howard?"

"What?"

"You got your wish. We aren't friends anymore. I don't want to be friends with such a wimp," she declared, tears filling her eyes. Before she could cry in front of him, she picked up the boot and shoved it at his chest.

He grabbed the boot, and the snake got frightened and slithered through his hands. He eased the snake back in the boot, staring at Sonya in surprise. Then she stomped up the cabin steps and slammed the door behind her.

Chapter Twelve

"Girls!" called the camp director from the steps of the dining hall.

Everyone stopped talking to listen.

"This morning's scavenger hunt will be girls against boys—Camp Long River versus Camp Honeywell," he explained. "You will each have a partner, and the partners will each have a list of items to be found."

"Sounds easy," said Sonya, who was happy to do anything after the day spent in the cabin.

"Okay, partners are Sonya Plummer and Lauren Tompkins, Dawn Selby and Terri Rivera, Monique Whitney and Angela King. . . ."

"Oh, no!" Sonya clapped her hands to her face. She turned and stared directly at Lauren, who only scowled back at her.

" 'Oh, no,' is absolutely right," said Lauren, walking over to stand beside Sonya. "I don't know how we got stuck with each other."

"Me, either."

Sonya's friends wore expressions of sympathy.

"Poor Sonya," said Dawn.

Then Merrie handed out the lists. There were four different items on each person's list.

Sonya gazed at her list. "Four-leaf clover, a piece of pyrite rock, a fish hook, an animal bone."

"We'll never find this stuff!" declared Angela.

"Where in the world will we find fish bones?" Wanda asked.

"Or blue lupins?" asked Monique, looking at her list.

"I guess this means hiking again," said Terri.

"I sure hope we don't have to go on a twenty-mile hike to find these dumb things," grumbled Lauren.

"Come on, get started," said Merrie. "Okay, you've been here long enough to know where to find the things on your lists. They're not exactly easy to find, but if you've been paying attention to our talks, you'll know what they are and where to look. Whichever camp returns with the most items wins. Okay, ready, set, go! Good luck!"

Girls fanned out from the campground in all directions. Sonya and Lauren walked toward the river.

"Why are we going this way?" asked Lauren.

"Because it's a good place to find fish hooks and rocks," explained Sonya. "We'll look in the river for a piece of pyrite."

"Okay. What does it look like?" asked Lauren.

Sonya stopped and stared at her. "Don't you remember our campfire talk on rocks? It's that

sparkly rock that winks at you. You can't miss it. It's
all over the place, but you'll see it better in water.''

"Except when you *have* to find it,'' Lauren pointed
out, staring glumly into the shallow part of the river.

They walked on for a while but didn't find
anything.

"I don't see the point of all this, you know?'' said
Lauren. "I mean, if they sent us looking for gold,
maybe that would make sense. But why are we looking for a worthless rock and dumb stuff like fish
hooks?''

"It's just a contest,'' said Sonya. "We don't have
to take it seriously.''

"Right, except if we lose, we'll have to clean up
after those boys,'' Lauren said. "This is bor-ing.''

"Come on, Lauren, it could be fun.'' Sonya wasn't
sure how anything could be fun with Lauren around,
but she had to try at least.

After fifteen more minutes Lauren stopped in her
tracks. "I think we should split up. I'll look for the
four-leaf clover and the rock. You can look for the
other stuff.''

"Sounds fair to me,'' said Sonya, relieved to be
able to be on her own. "I'm going to take a rowboat
downriver.''

"Okay, I'll meet you back at the dock after I've
found everything,'' said Lauren.

Sonya waved good-bye and ran back to the dock.
Carefully she loosened the line that held the boat to
the dock and pushed off, then jumped into the boat.
Finally she was free!

She rowed briskly downriver, enjoying the wind in her hair and the steady clunking of the oars turning in the oarlocks. She decided she would stop just downstream to look for the clover and animal bone.

Just then the wind and the current began to pull her to the center of the river toward the tiny island. She saw nothing but a few trees on the island—but then, looking closer, she saw someone there, waving frantically at her!

"Hey, stop! Help!" a boy's voice cried.

Sonya didn't recognize the voice—the wind made it sound foreign. She rowed closer to get a better look.

"Hey, over here!"

As she squinted her eyes, she saw a familiar face. Howard! Quickly she rowed up to the edge of the island.

"What are you doing here?" she exclaimed. "Did your boat sink?"

"No," Howard replied indignantly. "The boys left me here. A practical joke, I guess."

"That's too bad," said Sonya, but she didn't really feel sorry for him. She thought he deserved everything that happened to him.

He started to get into the boat.

"Hey, where do you think you're going?" asked Sonya. "Did I say I'd give you a ride?"

"No, but I just thought you stopped for me," Howard said. "I'm stranded on this island."

"And you thought I'd rescue you?" Sonya glared at him.

"Yeah. Well, why not?"

"Why not? Because you wouldn't rescue me if I was the one stuck on this dumb island," she told him.

"I would, too," Howard insisted, one foot still in the boat. "What kind of person do you think I am?"

"A selfish, snotty, mean one," Sonya said. She pulled the boat closer to shore and heard a clunk underneath it.

"Great, just great." Howard fumed, poking his walking stick into the boat. "So you'll just leave me out here to rot."

"Something like that," Sonya said.

"Look, if you don't rescue me, who knows how long I'll be out here," said Howard. "It could be a long time before anyone rows down this river."

Sonya looked up at the sky. Storm clouds were gathering. Howard was right. Nobody was going to row in the rain. "All right, but on one condition."

"What's that?" he asked eagerly.

"Apologize for everything," she insisted. "For all the stuff you've said about me."

"Sonya, I didn't mean any of it," he said. "I apologize, I really do."

"Okay." Sonya held out her hand to him to help him into the boat.

Just then Howard stabbed his walking stick into the boat, piercing a small hole in the bottom of it. Sonya saw what had happened and shrieked.

"You ruined my boat—on purpose!" she cried. "Now nobody can go anywhere—it's got a hole!"

"I'm sorry, really, I didn't mean to," said Howard, withdrawing the stick. "How could a stick do that?"

"You did it," accused Sonya. "You wanted to make sure I didn't leave without you, so you ruined my boat."

"Why would I do that, Sonya, if I wanted to leave, too?" Howard pointed out. "Do you think I'm crazy?"

"Yes," she said. She got out of the boat and tried to stuff her windbreaker in the hole to patch it. "I don't know how I'm going to fix this."

"Look, we'll think of something, don't worry," said Howard.

"But we could lose the scavenger hunt if I don't hurry up!" she cried.

"Oh, that," said Howard, shaking his head. He started pulling the boat onto the shore. There was another clunk. Howard took his tennis shoes off and waded into the water, digging around with his hand. "Wait. Your boat ran into something. It's a sharp metal thing and it must have struck your boat before I did."

"Oh, yeah?" Sonya drew up beside him and felt around in the water until she, too, grasped the sharp metal spike. "I'm sorry, Howard—really."

"Come on. Let's see what we can do with this boat."

Howard examined the hole. "I read somewhere that Native Americans used tree sap for a kind of glue."

"We've got plenty of sap around here," said

Sonya. "Usually I get it on me just walking in the woods."

She went over to one of the trees and scraped sap off the bark with her penknife.

"We can use your windbreaker," suggested Howard, laying it flat in the boat. He started to rip off the pocket.

"Hey, don't! My mom will kill me!" Sonya cried, grabbing it from him.

"But it's waterproof," insisted Howard. "I'll buy you another one. Just explain that you were stranded on a deserted island."

"With a strange boy," Sonya added. She laid the windbreaker pocket over the hole, and Howard applied sap around the edges of the pocket as though it were glue.

"Let's let it dry for about fifteen minutes, then we'll come back and launch the boat," said Howard.

They walked around the island, which was so tiny it only took one minute to do. Then they went back to the boat.

"The sap isn't really hard, but let's try it anyway," said Howard. He pushed the boat into the river, being careful to avoid the underwater metal spike, which was part of an old chain to tie a boat up to.

Sonya jumped in and Howard followed, bringing the line in behind him.

"It's leaking!" cried Sonya, watching water seep in under the waterproof pocket.

"Oh, no!" Howard used his hands as a cup to bail out the boat.

"It's filling too fast!" Sonya exclaimed. She used a small plastic bucket to scoop water out, but it was no use.

At that moment it started to rain. They pulled the boat onto the sand and ran for cover under some trees.

"I guess we're stuck here," said Sonya miserably.

Howard turned to her. "I'm really sorry, Sonya."

"Yeah, me, too. But it's not really your fault." Sonya squeezed water out of her shorts.

The rain stopped as suddenly as it had begun, and the sun emerged from behind some clouds. A rainbow curved across the river.

Howard squinted and pointed down the river. "Hey what's that?"

Sonya peered past the rainbow. In the distance a rowboat was moving toward them.

She jumped up and ran toward the shore. "Someone's come to rescue us!" Wildly she waved her hands in the air to get their attention.

"Hey, we're over here!" cried Howard, suddenly at her side.

"Oh, no—it's the boys!" Sonya shouted.

"I bet they won't pick me up—they don't like me," Howard said miserably.

"Of course they do," insisted Sonya. "They probably just like to tease you. Anyway, with friends like them, who needs enemies?"

Howard shrugged, but he didn't look convinced.

Finally the boys pulled the rowboat up on the bank. Robbie was in the lead, and he grinned at Howard.

"Hey, I didn't know you were hanging out here with your girlfriend, Howie," he said.

The other boys started laughing.

"Shut up," Howard hissed through his teeth.

"Leave him alone," said Sonya.

"Did you guys come to get me or not?" asked Howard.

"Sure. Are you bringing your girlfriend along?" asked Robbie, giving Sonya a weird look.

Sonya glared at him.

Howard looked at Sonya, then back at Robbie, as if confused.

She didn't want Howard to be teased anymore. "Look, go ahead. Someone will come for me," she told him quietly.

He frowned, then shook his head. "No way. We'll take you back to camp, too, Sonya."

She was surprised. The other boys stared at him, too.

"We're gonna have a girl in the boat?" one boy asked, then started laughing.

"Hey, it's not funny," said Robbie.

"Let's hear it for Howard!" cried Maurice, and everyone cheered.

"Howard Tartar Sauce, hooray!" shouted Robbie. The boys crowded around and slapped Howard on the back so hard he nearly fell over.

"Okay, guys. Enough's enough," said Howard, but he was grinning.

As Sonya and Howard climbed into the boat,

Sonya said, "See, Howard? They *do* like you. You just couldn't tell."

"You really think so?" he asked.

"Yeah. Maybe they were mean to you at first because they didn't know you, but now they like you. Look at all the ways you figured out how to get back at us and beat us in the wars. They wouldn't have thought of those things without you. They tease you because they like you and they know you're smart," explained Sonya.

Howard smiled warmly. "Hey, Sonya. Thanks for rescuing me. You were brave."

She grew warm all over. "I didn't do anything."

"Yeah, but you stayed with me even after I was a pain. I'm sorry for everything," he told her, secretly taking her hand in his.

Sonya smiled and stared around at the boys in the boat with them. Everything seemed fine now. Howard had stuck up for her after all.

"It's all your fault," declared Lauren hotly, standing in front of Cabin 4.

"What's all my fault?" asked Sonya as she approached, holding hands with Howard.

"It was your bright idea to split up, and look what happened to me!" Lauren was covered with tiny red scratches and looked like she was getting a rash.

"What happened to you?" asked Howard.

"I fell into a bunch of poison oak!" cried Lauren.

Sonya put her hand over her mouth to stop herself

from reminding Lauren that it was Lauren's idea to split up.

"And we lost the scavenger hunt. I found a four-leaf clover, though," Lauren added.

"That means today's your lucky day—you're going to get to take a shower," said Sonya.

"What?"

Sonya winked at Howard. Together they lifted Lauren and carried her, screaming, to the bath house. Howard held her while Sonya turned on the shower to all cold. Then Sonya rubbed baking soda on Lauren's arms. "Baking soda keeps you from getting poison oak really badly," Sonya explained. Lauren was still wearing her clothes.

"I'm freezing!" declared Lauren, while Sonya and Howard dunked Lauren's head in the water, getting almost as wet as she was.

That night Sonya and Howard sat together under an old moth-eaten blanket at the campfire, singing songs. Across from them sat Terri, Dawn, Angela, and Monique, who were glad to see Sonya back with Howard again.

The flames seemed to light up Howard's face as he suddenly motioned to Sonya to follow him. She got up and they stood in the darkness of the trees where no one could see them. Then Howard kissed her on the mouth.

Maybe we'll have that romance at camp, after all, thought Sonya happily.

About the Author

SUSAN SMITH was born in Great Britain and has lived most of her life in California and New York. She began writing when she was thirteen years old and has authored a number of novels for teenagers, including the *Samantha Slade* series by Archway Paperbacks. She is married and lives in Santa Fe, New Mexico, with her husband and three children. The children have provided her with many ideas and observations that she has included in her books. In addition to writing, Ms. Smith enjoys traveling, horseback riding, skiing, and swimming.

Look for Best Friends #16:

Angela and the Accidental On-Purpose Romance

coming in November 1991

Is there a recipe for romance? Angela is determined to find out. Her mom has just won an award for her cooking column. And Angela wants her to have a date for the big award ceremony. Angela enlists the help of her best friends to find the perfect date for Mrs. King—without her mom finding out they're playing Cupid, of course! It seems like Angela's found the perfect guy for her mom—until Jennifer's mother steals him away! Angela is furious at Jennifer. Meanwhile, it looks like Bobby Bugrin has a new girlfriend. The best friends are determined to come up with a new plan before Angela gives up on romance forever!